MY HERO A
S

MY HERO ACADEMIA

SCHOOL BRIEFS

4

ORIGINAL STORY BY
KOHEI HORIKOSHI

WRITTEN BY
ANRI YOSHI

Festival For All

U.A. HIGH SCHOOL

Hero Course: Class 1-A

Izuku Midoriya

Birthday: July 15
Quirk: One For All

Katsuki Bakugo

Birthday: April 20
Quirk: Explosion

Shoto Todoroki

Birthday: January 11
Quirk:
Half-Cold Half-Hot

Tenya Ida

Birthday: August 22
Quirk: Engine

Fumikage Tokoyami

Birthday: October 30
Quirk: Dark Shadow

Minoru Mineta

Birthday: October 8
Quirk: Pop Off

Ochaco Uraraka

Birthday:
December 27
Quirk: Zero Gravity

Momo Yaoyorozu

Birthday:
September 23
Quirk: Creation

Tsuyu Asui

Birthday: February 12
Quirk: Frog

Yuga Aoyama

Birthday: May 30
Quirk: Navel Laser

Mina Ashido

Birthday: July 30
Quirk: Acid

Mashirao Ojiro

Birthday: May 28
Quirk: Tail

Denki Kaminari

Birthday: June 29
Quirk: Electrification

Eijiro Kirishima

Birthday: October 16
Quirk: Hardening

Koji Koda

Birthday: February 1
Quirk: Anivoice

Rikido Sato

Birthday: June 19
Quirk: Sugar Rush

Mezo Shoji

Birthday: February 15
Quirk: Dupli-Arms

Kyoka Jiro

Birthday: August 1
Quirk: Earphone Jack

Hanta Sero

Birthday: July 28
Quirk: Tape

Toru Hagakure

Birthday: June 16
Quirk: Invisibility

Hero Course: Class 1-B

Itsuka Kendo

Birthday:
September 9
Quirk: Big Fist

Neito Monoma

Birthday: May 13
Quirk: Copy

Tetsutetsu Tetsutetsu

Birthday: October 16
Quirk: Steel

Ibara Shiozaki

Birthday:
September 8
Quirk: Vines

Yui Kodai

Birthday:
December 19
Quirk: Size

Reiko Yanagi

Birthday: February 11
Quirk: Poltergeist

Nirengeki Shoda

Birthday: February 2
Quirk: Twin Impact

Setsuna Tokage

Birthday: October 13
Quirk:
Lizard Tail Splitter

Yosetsu Awase

Birthday: November 7
Quirk: Weld

Hiryu Rin

Birthday: July 14
Quirk: Scales

General Studies

Hitoshi Shinso

Birthday: July 1
Quirk: Brainwashing

Support Course

Mei Hatsume

Birthday: April 18
Quirk: Zoom

MY HERO ACADEMIA

SCHOOL BRIEFS

4

CONTENTS

Festival For All

Part 1
Float-Filled Work Study

"Thank you again, for this! And see you tomorrow!" said Izuku Midoriya with a deep yet fidgety bow. He closed the door and stepped into the corridor, where Mirio Togata greeted him with a beaming, relaxed smile.

"Ah ha ha ha! So stiff, so rigid, Midoriya! You got approved by Sir, so cheer up, buttercup!" said the third-year boy.

"But, Togata... I dunno if I should really be celebrating..."

The students of U.A. High School had spent their summer adjusting to dorm life, and today was the first day of fall. These two were at Sir Nighteye's hero agency, about an hour's train ride away from U.A. Having successfully earned his provisional hero license, Midoriya now sought to learn a thing or two through a work study with All Might's former sidekick, and since Togata had already been working with Nighteye, the older boy had tagged along to make the introduction.

Though Nighteye had accepted Midoriya's application in the end, the strict hero hadn't deemed the boy a worthy successor of All Might's "One For All" Quirk, and he was determined to make Midoriya see things his way. What's more, Midoriya had failed to steal Nighteye's personal seal within three minutes (a task Nighteye had given him as a test of his abilities) and hadn't even been able to make Nighteye laugh, which had been Togata's suggestion at the start.

"I put everything I had into that All Might impression...and it flopped..." said Midoriya.

"It sure did! Swing and a miss!" agreed Togata jovially.

"Ugh..." groaned Midoriya, slumping over.

Midoriya wasn't usually one to fall into a funk, but his misfire of a joke haunted him. And what's more,

Nighteye had informed him that Togata had actually been the original candidate to inherit One For All. The fact that All Might had never mentioned this now weighed on Midoriya.

"But you two turned into total fanboys over All Might! Sir even seemed to enjoy it!" said Togata with a grin, unaware of Midoriya's inner turmoil.

"You really think so...?"

"Really, for real! I mean, I'm an All Might fan myself, but trivia like that is way outta my league."

Midoriya raised his eyes. Togata's comment got him thinking.

"That's understandable!" he said. "Not many people know about the Vinegar Suicide incident, but it's the perfect illustration of how All Might's actually a witty jokester! It's not just about having the strength to beat up villains, it's also about having the humanity and kindness—backed up by humor—to reassure those in need, like that half-drowned boy. They actually talk about it in the afterword of *All Might's Gags and Jokes: A Compendium*. How, like, his jokes have the cynical edge of American humor, while also being warm and relatable enough to inspire others..."

"He put out a jokebook, even? Who knew!"

"I saw it on Sir's bookshelf, actually. The revised edition. Oh, that reminds me! Didja see that tenth-anniversary tapestry? That one's so rare collectors refer to it as mythical merch. Or that life-size cardboard cutout! That was *never* mass-produced for the public, so it probably came from some invite-only celebration," continued Midoriya, the tinge of envy in his voice growing.

"Y'know, I hear that's not even Sir's whole collection," said Togata. "They say he's got a whole storage unit chock full of All Might merch."

"Whoaaa… You think he'd let me live in there?"

"Unlikely, but maybe you could get a peek?" said Togata with a straight face, but now that the topic had turned to All Might merchandise, Midoriya was off and running. As the excitable first-year blathered on, Togata took a good look at him and started thinking about Sir Nighteye. While on the job, the hero was impenetrable, with a glare as sharp as a knife, but off the clock, he would watch old clips of All Might and let those stern features relax, if only a little. Nighteye was and always had been a big fan of All Might, even

though the two had had a falling out several years ago.

Sir and Midoriya… They're more alike than they know.

Togata realized that, despite their radically different ways of showing it, the mentor and his new mentee both idolized All Might. That must mean they had some fundamental things in common, right? Hopefully, that common ground would lead to a good working relationship.

"And then there was… Huh? Togata? What's wrong?" said Midoriya, snapping Togata out of his thoughts.

"Nah, nothing. But, hey—I hope you're ready to give it your all starting tomorrow!"

UA

While Togata reflected on those two devotees of the All Might gospel, Fumikage Tokoyami was down in Fukuoka, doing his own work study with Hawks.

"Tick, tock," said the hero.

By the time Tokoyami got to the roof of the building, an impatient Hawks had already captured the villain that he and his team were after. The boy was getting used to the sight of prepackaged villains, tied and bound by Hawks, ready for processing. The police and other sidekicks arrived moments later to take the villain into custody.

"How about we take a breather?" suggested Hawks, passing out soft drinks to his team. One of the sidekicks asked when the boss had had the time to buy refreshments, so Hawks explained that during the chase, he'd rescued a lost child, and the grateful parent had offered the drinks as a reward.

Like they say, he's almost too *fast…*

Tokoyami used this brief respite to have a seat and think. Hawks's Quirk, "Fierce Wings," allowed him to multitask at top speed, and his efforts had made him a top-ten hero as a teen—the youngest ever to pull off that feat. Hence his reputation for excess speed in all things.

Tokoyami was doing a better job keeping up with the winged hero than he had several months before back during his internship, but at the end of the day, there was no measuring up to a man who could soar through the skies with ease.

"So, what's Endeavor's kid like?"

Tokoyami's eyes grew wide at the out-of-the-blue question from Hawks, who'd stealthily sat down next to the boy. Shoto Todoroki was, of course, Tokoyami's classmate and the son of the provisional number one hero, Endeavor. Though Tokoyami didn't know the specifics, it was obvious from Todoroki's attitude how little he cared for his fiery father.

"He's extremely capable," said Tokoyami, after some thought. "He excels both inside the classroom and out."

"Hmm. And personalitywise, he's just like his old man, I'm guessing?" said Hawks.

"No. He tends to be cool, calm, and collected, actually."

Hawks must've found something funny about this answer, since he replied with an intrigued grin and an amused "Ooh." Tokoyami squinted, wondering why his mentor was so curious about the Todoroki family. This didn't go unnoticed by Hawks.

"It's just that I'm a fan of Endeavor," he said with a laugh, reading Tokoyami's expression. His smile seemed childish with a hidden edge of cunning, but he cloaked himself in his broad red wings before Tokoyami could get a closer look.

UA

"Hey, hey, didja hear? Lunch Rush Sensei's got a limited-time tapioca milk rice bowl!"

"Yeah, I heard the rumors! I haven't had the courage to try it yet, though."

"What could it possibly taste like? Ribbit."

Nejire Hado, Ochaco Uraraka, and Tsuyu Asui were all doing their work study at Ryukyu's agency, and Hado's mention of the cafeteria's newest offering had the first-years doubting. They'd finished their work for the day, and now it was teatime; floral notes of jasmine and the sweet scent of cookies filled the office.

"Togata tried it and said it's tastier than you'd think," said Hado. "Like *ochazuke* filled with sweet little balls."

"That makes sense, but I'm still having a tough time imagining!" said Uraraka.

"It could be worth trying, at least once. Maybe. Ribbit," said Asui.

"Sounds like cutting-edge cuisine to me," said Ryukyu, watching over the three girls and their animated conver-

sation. Hado got up in the hero's face and said, "You'd eat it, right, Ryukyu? You totally would! Yeah! Yeah?"

"No, I think I'd pass," said Ryukyu with an awkward smile.

"Villain on the run on Espa Street," came a voice from the police scanner in the office. "Requesting immediate hero backup—"

In an instant, the relaxed mood evaporated. The four of them stood, ready for action. Teatime was over.

"With me, girls."

"Okaaay!" said Hado.

"Yes, ma'am," responded Uraraka and Asui in unison as they broke into a run.

A perfect portrait of a hero and her three gallant sidekicks.

UA

Meanwhile, Eijiro Kirishima's work study had brought him to one corner of Osaka.

"Got the tastiest *takoyaki* you'll find, over here! With the chunkiest octopus chunks in town!"

"*Okonomiyaki*! Get yer okonomiyaki here!"

"Here to see the *danjiri* festival floats? That pairs perfectly with our delish *horumonyaki*!"

The stall vendors hawked their street food with gusto, earning an impressed "Wow!" from Kirishima.

"I had no clue there'd be this much energy at my first-ever float festival!" he added.

This particular festival was famous nationwide, and it drew huge crowds. Naturally, crowds led to pickpocketing, squabbles, and full-blown fights, so heroes would do their part by patrolling during the festivities. Festivalgoers wore straight-sleeved *happi* coats representing whichever town they called home, and now they waited for the floats to start coming down the streets. Local pride was always on the line, and they would've given anything if it meant that their hometown float turned out faster and more glorious than the others, since this festival was the one time each year when they could really shine.

Next to Kirishima, Tamaki Amajiki yanked his costume's hood forward in an attempt to shield himself from the hustle and bustle.

"Ugh, festivals… Always so loud. Wild. Chaotic…"

"That's cuz it gets the blood pumping! Everyone's hyped as heck!" said Fat Gum with a hearty laugh, causing his tubby body to shake and jiggle. Kirishima and Amajiki were, of course, doing their work studies under the hero Fat Gum.

"Fat! Here, try our takoyaki!"

"'Preciate it!" said Fat Gum, taking the complimentary food from the hawker. The people of Osaka loved their hometown hero for his round body (which was not unlike a morsel of takoyaki) and general geniality—hence the nonstop stream of offers from those running the food stalls.

"Oh! I saw this youngster on the news!" said the hawker, glancing at Kirishima. "Your newest sidekick, right, Fat? Red Riot, was it? You were great out there, kid! Have some extra green onion topping, on the house! And give your gloomy pal some takoyaki, too! Maybe it'll put a bit of pep in his step!"

"Thanks a ton!" said Kirishima.

"Gloomy...?" muttered Amajiki, taken aback.

"Probably just cuz you've got your hood pulled up like that! Kinda dark, yeah? But don't sweat it, dude!" said Kirishima, trying to cheer up his friend. "And hey—your Quirk came back! That's great, huh!"

"Yeah…"

Fat Gum and the two boys had run into a gang of villains during the first patrol of their work study, and in the turmoil, Amajiki had been shot with a drug that had disabled his Quirk. Thankfully, the effects had worn off by the next day. Behind the scenes, Kai Chisaki and his Hassai Group were plotting to revive the yakuza, and part of the plan involved disseminating and testing the Quirk-killing drug created from the gang's boss's granddaughter, Eri, and her own Quirk. For now, though, Amajiki and Kirishima were blissfully unaware of these dark dealings. Fat Gum thought the whole thing seemed fishy, but all three were relieved that Amajiki's Quirk wasn't gone for good.

"Y'know, Tamaki, you'd be one heckuva hero if you could shake that doom 'n' gloom act," said Fat Gum, with a mouthful of takoyaki.

"The extra pressure doesn't help! I know about my issues better than anyone!" shot back Amajiki.

"That was totally a compliment, dude!" said Kirishima.

They kept patrolling the busy streets as they snacked on takoyaki, and the rich smells of sweet

sauces and grilling meat wafting from the stalls made their mouths water.

"Ooh, three of those beef skewers, mister! Plus, three *ikayaki*! And three *butaman* while you're at it, miss!"

"Whoa, Fat! I think I'm good!" said Kirishima in an attempt to pump the brakes, since Fat Gum couldn't help but order from every stall they passed.

"What's that? Full already?" asked the hero.

"Nah, not ready to burst, but it'll already be tough enough if we gotta break into a sprint or something... But hey—don't mind me! You keep chowing down!"

Fat Gum's Quirk, "Fat Absorption," gave him a body that could absorb attacks without taking damage. Villains caught by the blubber would quickly lose the will to resist, feeling as if they were sinking into the world's comfiest couch.

Amajiki's Quirk, on the other hand, was "Manifest," and it allowed him to reproduce features of whatever he'd eaten recently by making them sprout from his own body. In other words, for both him and Fat Gum, eating was just another part of the job. Still, after finishing his butaman, Amajiki nodded at Kirishima's assessment.

"Yeah, I think I've had enough variety today already."

"Couple a lightweights, you two!" said Fat. "Hey, mister! One choco-banana, if y'would!"

The heavyweight hero was just as partial to sweet as he was savory, and he scarfed down the banana in a single bite. It was a reasonable assumption that at the end of the day, he just loved eating.

"Hmm, with U.A. switching over to dorms and all, what're you kids doing for meals nowadays?" asked Fat Gum.

"Lunch Rush Sensei's food gets carted over to the dorms," said Kirishima. "We're free to cook for ourselves, of course, but most of us just go for the school food, cuz it's delish!"

"And there're plenty of options, too. All nutritious," added Amajiki with a small nod.

"Well, I gotta say—dorm life sounds like a hoot! Hanging out with your pals like it's a school trip every day," said Fat Gum.

"Feels pretty normal now that we're used to it, though I do have a blast getting to chat with everyone all the time! Right, Amajiki?" said Kirishima.

"I do have at least one good friend..." said Amajiki.

"Do fights ever break out?" asked Fat Gum.

"Actually, yeah. Happened the other day," said Kirishima, still scanning the area. "With these two guys in my class, who've known each other forever."

"Hah! Even at that elite school! Thought so!" said Fat Gum, whose eyes grew unexpectedly wide at Kirishima's answer.

"Right…" said Amajiki, remembering. "That's what had Hound Dog Sensei so worked up the other day…"

After Midoriya and Katsuki Bakugo had snuck out one night and started going at it, Hound Dog, the school life supervisor, had had some choice words for the student body at the opening ceremony for the new semester.

"But, dude, I'm telling ya, those two? There's always been bad juju between them… Bakugo and Midoriya, I mean," explained Kirishima.

"Hmm? The two from the Sports Festival, right?" said Fat Gum. "The one who beat himself up something fierce, and the one who took home the first-years' top prize? So those two're childhood buddies, huh?"

"Mirio had his eye on Midoriya… But I guess Bakugo was still on lockdown when Mirio sparred with your whole class?" asked Amajiki.

"Yup! Bakugo used to be spoiling for a fight all the time, but ever since he and Midoriya scrapped for real, he's been acting a little more housebroken!" said Kirishima with a grin, and Fat Gum shot back a smile of his own.

"It's a great thing, youth! How 'bout you, Tamaki? Ever duked it out with Mirio down by the riverside? I'm thinking…not?"

Amajiki returned the smile with a frown.

"No… We've never fought about anything."

"Get outta here! Not even an argument? And you've been pals since elementary?" asked Fat Gum.

"Neither of us ever did anything worth fighting about, I guess…" said Amajiki.

"Nah, I get it, though. Mirio's just such a cheery dude all the time," said Kirishima.

"Yeah… He's pretty amazing, honestly," added Amajiki, smiling as if Kirishima's compliment had somehow been aimed at him. Kirishima thought of Bakugo and Midoriya again, and how he hadn't once witnessed them engage in polite conversation since school started. And if they ever did? It'd be the talk of class A for days.

Whatever! Friends, frenemies—it takes all types, I guess!

Kirishima dropped the comparison in his mind, admitting to himself that some people just weren't destined to get along. Even those with seemingly rocky relationships might get on better than the rest of the world knew, so it wasn't his place to expect identical friendships from every pair.

"Bakugo's just the type to explode and tell you how he really feels," said Kirishima.

"Meaning...?" said Amajiki.

"The way I see it, he's honest with himself!" said Kirishima with a grin.

As they talked, one especially gaudy float on the roadside caught Kirishima's eye; the handlers were hard at work preparing, since it was nearly time for the parade. From what Kirishima had heard, these portable shrine floats were three to four meters tall and weighed about four tons. While the handlers towed the shrine on wheels, a designated cartwright would dance on the roof with *uchiwa* fans and shout directions to the handlers. These cartwrights were the real stars who gave energy to the festival, as they had to maintain their balance while the floats zoomed down the streets at high speed.

As the trio oohed and aahed, a young cartwright clambered onto the roof of the float. He had chiseled features and an equally chiseled physique under his distinctive happi coat, and the heroic pose he struck elicited cheers from his squad mates, who all wore matching happi.

"Looking gooood, Little Ei!"

"Yeah! You're rocking it!"

"Erm, thanks?" blurted Kirishima, who'd also been called "Ei" during his middle school days. The float squad turned to him in confusion, and he explained the misunderstanding in a hurry.

"Sorry, I also go by Ei, so I thought you meant me!"

"I've got the same nickname as a hero? What an honor!" said the young cartwright, beaming and shooting his hands into the air. Kirishima thought he seemed like a decent guy. The rest of the squad thanked the trio for patrolling during the festival, and though they seemed a little rough around the edges, they were all as good natured as the cartwright.

"Give 'em hell out there, mister!" shouted Kirishima toward the young man on the roof.

"Will do!"

Fat Gum and the boys couldn't stay in one spot too long, but as they turned to leave, they heard a shout from behind.

"You okay, Little Ei?"

"Getting nervous, buddy?"

The young cartwright must have slipped, because he was now sitting awkwardly on the roof, bracing himself with his arms.

"Y-you morons! Me? Nervous? On today of all days? Naw, someone left a banana peel up here, is all!"

"Oof! That's twice you've flopped, Little Ei! First, flat on your ass, and then with that dud of a joke!"

"Wow, that's the thanks I get for trying to calm all of *your* nerves with some classic humor!" said the cartwright with a laugh as he stood back up on the roof. Kirishima could sense that something was amiss, and he noticed that the cartwright's legs were trembling. His intuition was more spot on than he knew.

UA

"I've got some business to attend to, so you two take a break, okay?"

After a bit more patrolling, Fat Gum was summoned to police headquarters, so Kirishima and Amajiki snuck away from the crowds, got some drinks, and found a spot in an alley to rest.

"Nothing beats fruit punch," said Kirishima.

"And since they put milk in it here in Osaka, it's kind of creamy," said Amajiki.

"Milk, huh? Does that mean you'll be able to manifest cow parts now?"

"Of course."

"What about the fruit, though?"

Before Amajiki could answer, the boys heard a familiar voice.

"I'm really, really sorry for all that, back then..."

Nearby, the young cartwright from earlier was bowing in apology to a mother and her child—a boy of about five.

"Never you mind! We know it was an accident, and my boy's been all healed up for ages now. Isn't that right, Ken?"

"Yeah! Doesn't even hurt at all when I run now! But hey, hey, Mister Ei, when's your float gonna come out?"

"We're fifth in line, I think..."

"Cool! Mom, let's go find a spot to watch, quick! Good luck, Mister Ei!"

With that, the pair left the alley, the boy tugging impatiently on his mother's hand. The cartwright saw them off with a pained look that showed no trace of his earlier bravado.

"Hey, isn't he...?" said Kirishima.

"Yeah. From earlier..." said Amajiki.

They guessed that the young man probably didn't want to be seen in this state, so they hesitated to approach.

"Back I go, then..." said the cartwright to himself, but as he started to walk away, he slipped and fell on his rear.

"It really was a stinkin' banana peel this time!" he said, quipping to no one in particular.

"Leave it to Osaka, the capital of comedy!" said Kirishima, staring at the fruit peel in disbelief.

"It probably came from one of those choco-banana stalls," said Amajiki, offering a reasoned take that satisfied Kirishima. The cartwright finally noticed the boys and gave them a weak smile.

"Ha ha... You fellas aren't seeing my best side today, I swear..."

"Um, are you hurt, mister?" asked Kirishima,

lending the cartwright a hand. Both boys noticed that his legs were trembling again, and upon noticing that they'd noticed, he fell silent.

"So, what happened, exactly?" asked Kirishima, unable to resist after everything he'd seen. The question made the cartwright's face crumple like that of a child on the verge of tears, but sometimes it was a hero's job to meddle.

"Being a cartwright... It was always my dream," explained the young man haltingly, clearly unused to telling his story. "And last year, that dream of mine finally came true... But..."

During his first festival as cartwright, the previous year, he'd given the squad a badly timed cue and accidentally sent the float toppling over, hurting little Ken in the process. It wasn't a major injury, and the family had accepted the float squad's profuse apology, but as this year's festival approached, Ei the cartwright couldn't help but brood about the incident.

"I was fine all during practice, but now that today's the day… What if I hurt someone else? And slipping earlier like that… I'm a mess," he said with a clear tremor in his voice, despite his best efforts to remain composed.

Kirishima and Amajiki listened to the tale attentively.

Even when up against bloodthirsty villains, heroes had a duty to fight for justice without taking lives. They must also be keenly aware of their surroundings at all times to prevent bystanders from coming to harm. Heroes could brush off their own injuries, but more than anything, they feared hurting others. In this sense, Kirishima and Amajiki saw in the cartwright not a simple coward, but someone doing his best to be kind and strong. It got Kirishima thinking about his own experiences during middle school.

He had idolized Crimson Riot—a hero who stood for chivalry—and had been inspired enough to set his sights on becoming a hero himself. In Kirishima's quest to embody that chivalrous spirit, he had stuck his neck out for the bullied and honed his body until it was strong enough to defend the meek, but his relatively unremarkable "Hardening" Quirk was a sore spot that had left him lacking confidence.

One day, an ominous giant with a radio hanging from his neck had shown up in the neighborhood and asked some of Kirishima's schoolmates for directions. The girls had found themselves paralyzed by instinctual fear, as the giant exuded an unsettling, palpable, almost toxic bloodlust.

Kirishima had known he had to act, but he'd found his feet glued to the pavement by that same terror, even with the teary-eyed girls just a stone's throw away. Where he'd been unable to do a thing, another schoolmate—Mina Ashido—had. Despite her own fear, she had leaped between the giant and his would-be victims.

It was around that time that Kirishima had seen a similar incident on the news, when a middle schooler from somewhere or other had been captured by a powerful villain. That boy, too, had had a classmate who was willing to dive into action on the slim hope of saving his friend, so clearly there were people out there who could dash headlong into danger when lives were on the line. Meanwhile, Kirishima himself hadn't been able to move a muscle.

It had crushed him. Made him feel small, weak, and

pathetic, and he'd been reckoning with that shame ever since.

"I get it, mister. I've been paralyzed by that same sorta fear before," said Kirishima to the cartwright.

Amajiki looked a little shocked to hear this.

"But it's like Crimson Riot said—villains're scary and dying's scary, but the scariest of all is not saving a life that you could've... For me, I can't afford to stay scared and let that stop me. Cuz being chivalrous means...there are times when you gotta swallow that fear and pretend everything's A-OK anyway."

At Kirishima's earnest words, the cartwright paused and then gave a small smile.

"I'm a fan of Crimson Riot too, y'know. But... turning those ideals into reality ain't so easy..." he said.

"Aw, c'mon, Mister Ei..." said Kirishima in protest.

"Naw, I can't, I won't... I hate to do it, but I'm gonna tell them they gotta find another cartwright."

"But why?"

"It's been on my mind for a while. Quitting, that is. Just cuz it's my dream doesn't mean I'm the man for the job, and I'd rather get outta the game before I get someone else hurt. So thanks, but no thanks."

The cartwright gave the boys one last weak smile before walking away. Kirishima stood speechless, until he realized that his own failed pep talk had driven the cartwright to this drastic decision.

"I need to work on my speeches!" he cried, punching himself in the arm and leaving Amajiki to catch the can of juice that went flying.

"That wasn't the takeaway I wanted! Stay put, Amajiki—I'll be right back!"

"Still hoping to convince the guy?" asked Amajiki. "He's not in a place where your words will reach him right now…"

"I still gotta try!"

"Listen, if he's gonna take that next step, he's got to find the conviction himself. Giving someone an encouraging push from behind is a nice sentiment, but unless they're prepared to start marching forward, you'll just end up knocking them flat on their face."

Though his words might have sounded cold, Amajiki cast his gaze down almost apologetically.

Kirishima understood what his friend was saying— that the heart had to change before the body could act—but the thought of leaving well enough alone

set his teeth on edge. After all, he still hadn't quite overcome that moment of fear in his past.

"Ugh, I just gotta!" he said, but before Kirishima could start running, Fat Gum's voice came through on the boys' earpieces.

"Tamaki, Kirishima, hurry on over to police headquarters! We got us a sitch!"

[A]

About half an hour later, Kirishima and Amajiki were back on patrol, but this time they were clad in festival-appropriate happi coats of their own. With his muscled body boldly exposed, Kirishima was ready to blend in to the crowd like any other ordinary festivalgoer there to rep their hometown. Amajiki, on the other hand, wore his lack of confidence on his happi sleeves; his hunched posture meshed poorly with his festival attire and made him seem wildly out of place.

Hero costumes weren't an option, though, since the police had informed them that a villain suspected of bank robbery had come to town for the float festival.

The mission: to go undercover and search for the robber amid the hubbub. Fat Gum's massive frame gave him away no matter his garb, so he would be off patrolling on his own for the time being.

"This doesn't feel right for me…" said Amajiki.

"Just cheer up, put on a happy face, and that happi'll suit you just fine!" said Kirishima.

"'Cheer up,' huh? Easier said than done…"

The boys heard a raucous cheer from a few blocks away. The thunderous roar of the crowd, animated shouting, and accompanying music were all drawing closer.

"The float parade must be starting," said Amajiki, but before Kirishima could respond, the float that was earning those cheers zoomed past the two boys. It was a big one, with about a dozen men riding on all sides. The cartwright on the roof bounced along to the music and shouted directions, while the others were responsible for breaking, steering, or banging on bells and *taiko* drums. On the ground, several dozen men were either pulling the float from the front or pushing it from the back. Trailing behind the float were fellow revelers from the same hometown, running and whooping. With their sheer energy, the whole squad

and the float itself seemed to meld and transform into an enormous runaway beast.

"Lookit them go!" cried Kirishima.

Another twenty or so floats whizzed by, each one whipping the crowd into more of a mad frenzy and adding to the don't-blink-or-you'll-miss-it spectacle of it all. Leading the charge and looking down on the audience from up high were the cartwrights. Kirishima realized he might've gone for that job, if he'd been born in these parts.

"Hrm."

He remembered Ei the cartwright and grimaced.

"Let's keep moving," said Amajiki, forcing Kirishima to buck up. Whether they saw action or not, the boys were already on the job as heroes in training.

"Average height, average weight, plain face…" said Kirishima, going over the intel they'd received on the bank robber. "No distinguishing features at all, really… Finding this dude in the crowd could be tough!"

The official start of the parade only drew more onlookers, to the point that even snaking through the crowd was now a challenge.

"What kind of wanted criminal shows up at a

festival? This guy must really have a thing for these floats," said Amajiki, already getting fed up. The intel did indeed suggest that the villain they were after was fond of the float festival.

"I kinda get it, though! This is like nothing else! Hmm? Where're you headed, Amajiki?"

"Let's just split up," suggested Amajiki as the ebb and flow of the crowd yanked him away from Kirishima. The latter nodded and turned to move in the other direction while scanning the faces.

"You got some nerve, guy! Who goes around bumping into people and doesn't even say sorry?"

A woman was shouting.

"Wasn't on purpose, idiot!"

A man spat back.

The voices were close by, so Kirishima wove through the crowd while apologizing. The task at hand was finding a wanted criminal, but handling smaller disputes was still part of the job description.

"Look—takoyaki sauce all over my top!"

"Not my problem, lady. I'm risking everything to see these damn floats, so just buzz off!"

"How dare you! Somebody, call for a hero!"

"Right here, ma'am!" said Kirishima. "What seems to be the problem?"

As he approached the pair, the older man who'd been arguing with the young woman whipped around.

"No problem here, kid, so get outta my face!"

Average height, average weight, no distinguishing features.

"You're a wanted villain!" shouted Kirishima before he could stop himself. The man's face seemed to cloud over, and a thick layer of gelatin suddenly coated his entire body. Kirishima was already midlunge, but the gelatinous man slipped right through his hands and started bouncing away, over the heads of the crowd.

"Dude's got a jellifying Quirk!"

In a panic, Kirishima requested backup from Amajiki and Fat Gum and shoved past the crowd into the street itself, where he started chasing down the jellied villain.

"Surrender, you!"

"Ugh... You wanna play hardball?"

"Eek!"

The cry came from Ken—the boy injured by Ei's float the previous year—who had now become the unfor-

tunate hostage of the runaway villain. Before Kirishima could react, the villain shoved Ken into his own layer of gelatin and pointed a knife at the boy's stomach.

"One more step, and the kid gets it in the gut!"

Ken's mother and the nearby onlookers started screaming. Behind this group in the street, an approaching float managed to slow down and stop.

"Oh no... Is that Ken?" came the dumbfounded voice of Ei the cartwright, who had convinced one of his squad mates to take his place on the roof and was now riding at the back, on a lower level.

Ken himself flew into a panic and began squirming like mad.

"Sit still, brat! And, you—hero—if you want this kid to live to see tomorrow, you're gonna back the hell off!"

Once again, the jellied villain bounced into the air and starting tumbling through the crowd at top speed.

"Damn it!" cursed Kirishima, ignoring the villain's warning and taking off in pursuit without a second thought.

"A villain?"

"He's got a knife!"

"Some sorta maniac!

Panic spread through the crowd like wildfire, and before anyone knew it, the road was full of stampeding festivalgoers and floats alike. The villain was getting away, but Kirishima's path was blocked.

"Scuse me, folks! Could everyone just calm down and let me through?"

Though shouting at the top of his lungs, Kirishima couldn't cut through the madness of the mob, and within moments, the escaping villain had vanished from sight.

"Crud, what now?" he said, his face contorting in frustration.

"Hey! Hero! The villain's headed thataway!"

Legs still trembling, Ei the cartwright had climbed back onto the roof, putting the vantage point to good use. Kirishima heard the cartwright and struggled through the crowd to reach the float, where he bowed to Ei's panicked team and made his request.

"Please help me out, guys! We gotta save that little kid!"

Kirishima knew they had to act, and with the young cartwright scanning up top and him riding shotgun, they might figure out a way to chase down the villain.

"We just gotta clear a path somehow, right?" said

Ei, reading Kirishima's thoughts and thinking a step ahead. Without waiting for an answer, he took a deep breath and belted out orders to the crowd.

"You sorry bunch! Is this what Osakans are made of? If you're here to see the floats, then clear the damn road! That kid's life depends on it!"

Ei's roar echoed through the street, and the milling mob froze in place. Inspired by their young leader's daring act, the squad mates picked up their ropes and began urging people out of the way.

"Please, hero! Save that kid for me!" implored Ei once Kirishima had made it up to the roof. Shocked by this outpouring of help, Kirishima put a hand on Ei's shoulder, lifting his head from a deep bow.

"We're gonna save him together!"

With newfound reassurance and a solid ally at his side, Ei nodded, picked up his fans, and started shouting orders. The interim cartwright clapped Ei on the back before descending to a lower level, and the rope pullers finished their preparations, cried "Heave ho!" in unison, and started marching. Responding to the beat of the music and the float's powerful presence, the crowd parted like the Red Sea before Moses.

Ei the cartwright was a man in his element, leading

the charge. His squad mates grinned to see him back in action, and someone shouted, "We knew you had what it takes to be on top, Little Ei!" To have power on top, after all, you had to have good support from those down below.

While Ei kept his sights set on the runaway villain and made sure the speeding float was pointed in the right direction, Kirishima struggled to maintain his balance and fed updates to Fat Gum and Amajiki.

"Roger that, kid," said Fat over the comms piece.

"We hear you. But where are *you* right now, Kirishima?" asked Amajiki.

"Up on the float!"

"Say what?" said Fat Gum. "When'd you go native on us?"

The float flew around a curve without slowing down a beat. The handlers knew this city like the backs of their hands, and its winding streets weren't about to keep them from the escaping villain.

"I said, keep back!"

The villain was nearly in reach, but he once again had the knife pointed at Ken.

A moment's hesitation, and all could be lost.

Kirishima knew that, so he dove toward the

villain from atop the still-moving float, activated his Hardening in midair, and stole back the boy. The villain's knife connected, but instead of tearing into flesh, it glanced off the hardened skin of Kirishima's back and bounced away.

With his hostage lost, the villain applied another layer of gelatin and turned to make his getaway.

"Not so fast," murmured Amajiki, glaring at the villain.

The hero in training whipped out an arm resembling a squid tentacle—suckers and all—stretchy enough to reach the villain and strong enough to cut through the gelatin and bind him head to toe.

"Amajiki!"

But Kirishima wasn't able to admire his fellow mentee's handiwork for long.

"Watch out, hero!" cried Ei the cartwright. Kirishima turned to see the float barreling toward him. The emergency break took hold just in time, but the sudden stop rocked the float off balance and sent it listing forward.

Kirishima wrapped his hardened body around little Ken, prepared to take the hit, but the "crunch" he expected never came. Instead, he heard a much softer "fwump."

"Fat!"

Fat Gum's considerable heft had stopped the falling float.

"I keep making a habit of showing up late to the party, huh! Everyone okay?"

Kirishima checked Ken for bumps and bruises before saying, "Yup."

"Thanks!" said Ken, before dashing over to Ei the cartwright.

"You were so cool up there doing all that, Mister Ei! I wanna be a cartwright just like you someday!"

The cartwright's expression softened, and then the man fell to pieces, happier than words could express.

"Check it out, boys! Little Ei's crying his eyes out!" teased one of his squad mates, while the others looked on with wide smiles.

"Yeah, but only cuz your stench is stinging my eyes! You guys need a bath after all that running, yeesh!" shot back Ei, before turning to Kirishima.

"It was just like you said, hero—I couldn't let myself set such a bad example for this little guy."

"Hell yeah! You were supercool out there!" said Kirishima.

Ei the cartwright grinned, and Kirishima flashed him a trademark thumbs-up.

UA

With the villain in police custody and the chaos quelled, the festival was back on and Fat Gum and his two mentees were once again patrolling the street.

"Well, ain't that a story and a half," said the hero, after Kirishima filled him in on the earlier events as well as his own past failure.

"Listen, there are folks out there who got what it takes to dive into danger," continued Fat, "and others who don't. Just how it is, and it ain't our place to hold it against 'em."

"But…"

Kirishima wasn't quite ready to accept that that was "just how it was" sometimes, but Fat Gum read the boy's frustrated expression loud and clear.

"You wanted to act, but you couldn't, right?" said the hero, looking as serious as ever. "But clocks ain't made to be turned back, and all we can do is continue moving forward. You keep holding on to those regrets though, y'hear me, Kirishima? That ain't a bad thing."

"Yes, sir."

"It's your job not to forget how you felt back then, when you were feeling all pathetic, or scared, or weak, cuz that's your starting point. Your foundation. How're you gonna take the next step without a foundation, huh? There's no fooling yourself into being better than you are, not really. The guys who can get away with acting tough *know* they're tough, deep down."

As Kirishima digested his mentor's message, the roar of the crowd and jaunty music announced the coming of Ei the cartwright's float. As it passed by, Kirishima saw the proud face of a man who'd managed to take that next, essential step. A man whose legs were no longer trembling.

"Yes, sir!"

The look on Ei's face had given Kirishima the courage he needed to take his own next step. Just like Ashido. And just like that other, unnamed boy he'd seen on the news.

Maybe the other boy was hoping to be a hero too, and maybe Kirishima would cross paths with him

someday. If and when that day ever came, Kirishima wanted to be proud of the man he'd become.

Little did he know that he and that very boy were already classmates.

Prep

Kai Chisaki and the Hassai Group had plotted to use the Quirk-killing drug produced from Eri to rise to power, but their scheme had ended in failure when the hero team successfully stormed the yakuza compound and rescued the girl. This had come at a high price, however; Chisaki had killed Sir Nighteye, Mirio Togata had lost his Quirk, and Tomura Shigaraki and the League of Villains had managed to steal samples of the drug in question. These losses contributed to heavy criticism of law enforcement and growing dissatisfaction with the hero establishment from the public at large. Though emotions ran high all around in the immediate aftermath, time marched quietly onward, and the chill winds of the coming winter did much to soothe the wounds of all those involved.

Eri's Quirk could "rewind" living things to previous states, but as she couldn't yet control this powerful ability, she was quarantined in a hospital for the time being. That said, there was little worry of another rampage since the horn on her forehead that emitted the rewinding energy seemed to have shrunk since the big battle. She couldn't stay at the hospital forever, of course, so those in charge were in the process of deciding where she would end up. One proposal was U.A. High itself, because of the presence of none other than Shota Aizawa, whose "Erasure" Quirk was, for now, the only known check against potential outbursts of Eri's ability. Today, Aizawa was at the hospital for a visit.

"Umm..."

"What is it?"

The standard hospital bed dwarfed the small girl, who looked at Aizawa questioningly while sipping juice through a straw.

"What kinda dance is Deku gonna do...?"

A glint of anticipation shone in her eyes. Enthusiasm, even.

Ever since Eri's variant Quirk had manifested, her daily life had been nothing but pain. Though the six-year old's dark, brutal past still weighed on her and would not soon be forgotten, Izuku Midoriya had suggested that she attend U.A.'s upcoming School Festival. Aizawa thought that introducing her to the school on the day of the bombastic festival might be a bit much, so he'd brought Eri for a visit just a few days earlier and had witnessed her adjusting to life in the outside world, little by little. The sights and sounds of the older children working hard to prepare for the big event had already planted a seed of excitement in Eri's wounded heart, and their events, performances, and exhibits might be just the things to help that seed sprout.

"You can look forward to finding out, on the day of," said Aizawa.

Eri made a face far too serious for someone her age and, with a rapid series of small nods, said, "Okay... I'll look forward to it..." It was half in agreement, half in wonderment about the very concept of having anything at all to look forward to.

Though Aizawa had been taking a number of days off recently, he'd gotten word about how hard his kids were working. He was still a bit concerned how the other classes would respond to class A's bold plan, but he wasn't worried about the quality of the event itself. Whether working for others' sake or their own, the effort his students were putting in would be sure to reach hearts and minds.

A few days had passed since Aizawa's hospital visit. With U.A. High's dorm system firmly in place, the students' animated conversations and laughter filled the campus even on Sundays, and today was no exception. In fact, the grounds were even more active on this particular Sunday, since the kids had no time to lose in prepping for the impending festival. Weather this good made it the perfect day to roll up their sleeves and put in a full day's work.

In one grassy area near the main school building, class 1-C of General Studies was busy putting together its own exhibit, a haunted house they called "Labyrinth of Doom."

"Shinso, hold this up while I nail it in!"

"Sure thing."

Hitoshi Shinso put down the lumber he was carrying and approached his classmate, who was struggling to mount a grandfather clock against a wall. He held the clock in place, and each rap of the hammer against the nails made Shinso's muscular arms tingle.

"The clock looks good here, right, guys?" asked the classmate with the hammer. The others seemed to approve, but in Shinso's opinion, the stately clock looked almost too nice for what was supposed to be a decrepit mansion.

"Since the clock's going to start crying like a creepy baby, shouldn't it look a little more aged and worn down?" he said. His classmates thought about it, nodded, and started in with their own suggestions.

"Did we still have some of that paint lying around that makes wood look damaged?"

"Nope. None here."

"There should be a can back in the classroom, though."

"Hey, how about some baby handprints on the floor in front of the clock? With red paint! Spooky, right?"

"Totally creepsville!"

"And more handprints on the wall facing the clock! Just to up the creepy factor!"

"Nice thinking! That'll send those Hero Course kids crying for their mommies."

"Ooh, I've got it! Let's put some bloodstained diapers here and there, too!"

"How is that scary, exactly?"

While his classmates laughed and discussed ideas, Shinso picked up the unused lumber and said, "I can grab that paint after I take this to the trash." A number of them thanked him, and he walked away in silence.

Ever since he'd put in his transfer request, Shinso had started feeling pangs of guilt while hanging out with these familiar faces. When should he tell them? Would it be too late if he waited until his transfer was approved? Shinso was more aware than anyone that his "Brainwashing" Quirk wasn't suited to traditional hero work, but he'd decided to pursue his dream and apply to U.A. all the same. Unfortunately, the practical portion of the entrance exam (a battle against robots) hadn't been a stage where his talents could shine, and he had been rejected from the Hero Course. Shinso had anticipated this and submitted a separate application

to General Studies just in case, knowing that with good enough grades, an eventual transfer to the Hero Course was theoretically possible.

His outstanding performance in the Sports Festival had put the transfer plan into motion, but still, nothing was guaranteed, and he already perceived an enormous gap between himself and the students of the Hero Course who'd been training since the start of the school year. Until Shinso could receive that same training, it was up to him to work on his Quirk on his own time. Aizawa must've felt an affinity for the boy since he'd agreed to help in the meantime. Shinso understood the rare opportunity before him and would put up a desperate fight if that's what it took, but all the same, he was plagued by doubts and unease.

Shinso stopped, gazed up at the blue sky, and sighed. A cool breeze shepherded the clouds overhead.

Was there really a spot waiting for him in the Hero Course? Where would this next great leap land him? His doubts made him feel like one of those drifting clouds, and nothing scared Shinso more than being blown about into nothingness. It was this lack of confidence that had kept him from telling his current classmates about the possible transfer.

Now distinctly aware of his fainthearted turn, Shinso shook his head to dispel the dark thoughts before setting off for the classroom.

"Those balloons shaped like our teachers... Those positions look good to you?"

"I think you spelled something wrong on this sign!"

"The food stalls are sure to rake in the biggest profits."

"I hear 1-A's putting together some kinda band?"

"Kenranzaki's probably gonna pull off her third win in a row at the beauty pageant."

"Sucks that the teachers aren't doing anything special themselves, this year. I was looking forward to that."

As he walked across the campus, Shinso picked up conversations here and there, knowing that the energized atmosphere was only going to intensify as the festival approached. For any given high school in Japan, the ubiquitous school festival was a chance for students to let off some steam and learn a thing or two outside of the classroom. With that in mind, Shinso reflected on how this one might be his first and last with the members of class C. Feeling dark thoughts encroaching again, he put on his best poker face and

tried to focus on the simple act of walking. Rather than embrace the angst, why not concentrate on what he could and should do?

The trash collection spot was behind the main building, but as Shinso rounded the corner, he found himself staring at an enormous dragon on the nearby patch of grass. One big enough to ride.

Right… Class B is doing a play.

The students of class 1-B were hard at work painting the dragon's head and building set pieces resembling a castle, rocky crags, and so on.

"C'mon, Monoma, isn't this good enough?" said Yosetsu Awase. "It's as realistic as it's gonna get."

"Yes, we've covered the realism angle. Now we're going for sheer intensity," explained Neito Monoma.

Apparently Monoma wasn't quite satisfied with the already very impressive dragon prop.

"Let him have his way!" said Tetsutetsu Tetsu-tetsu, slapping the exasperated Awase on the back. "Attention to detail ain't a bad thing!"

"I knew you were a man of taste, Tetsutetsu," said Monoma, while adding intricate cross-hatching nearly too detailed to be done with a paintbrush.

"Ooh, that's looking great," said an impressed Setsuna Tokage, who was painting a crag nearby.

Proud of his handiwork and the positive reactions to it, Monoma threw back his head and laughed. "I daresay our dragon is nearly ready to devour class A whole! They can have their silly band and dance club, since everyone knows that the *theatrical production* is the tried-and-truest road to success at a school festival! Yes, it will be class B that claims the limelight this time!"

Shinso walked past class B, wondering if modern medicine had come up with a name for whatever disturbing condition was clearly afflicting Monoma.

If my transfer gets approved, I could end up as his classmate...

Shinso figured that he was more likely to be placed in class A—given Aizawa's involvement in his independent training—but class B was still a possibility. He wondered if he was getting ahead of himself, though.

A bit farther along the path, he came across Mina Ashido, Ochaco Uraraka, Tsuyu Asui, and the floating clothes of the invisible Toru Hagakure. Yes, class A's

dance squad was in the middle of practice, though Eijiro Kirishima, Minoru Mineta, Hanta Sero, Rikido Sato, Mezo Shoji, and Koji Koda sat off to the side, apparently taking a breather.

"I'm gonna lodge a complaint with the PTA!" shouted a fuming Mineta.

"Chill out, dude," said Kirishima, trying to calm his classmate. "I'm sure Sensei kept it a secret for a reason."

"We're talking the all-important notice about the beauty pageant! That's, like, as important as finding out if school's gonna be closed due to weather! I swear, I'm gonna give Sensei a piece of my mind for this dereliction of duty!"

"Yeah, riiight," teased Sero. "One glare from him and you'll fall to pieces, more like."

This earned a pouty scowl from Mineta.

"Sensei wasn't messing around," said Sato. "He was all like, 'Given how long you all took to decide on your event, I knew that informing you about the beauty pageant would only lead to more time wasting.'"

Sato punctuated his impression of Aizawa with a wide-eyed glare.

"'You got that, Mineta?'" said Sero, also imitating Aizawa's gravelly growl.

"Knock it off! You trying to make me wet myself again?" protested Mineta.

"Please don't have another 'accident,' Mineta," said Shoji.

"Har har, quit acting like it happens all the time, Shoji!"

As Mineta ranted, the big-boned Koda recalled Aizawa's tone and shuddered in fear.

This conversation got Shinso's attention. While Aizawa was stern enough during training, Shinso still hadn't experienced a full-blown scolding himself. Strangely enough, he almost felt jealous that the kids of class A had.

"Stop sitting on your butt and get back to work, Mineta!" said Mina, who'd just finished coordinating with the other girls.

"Yeah, this's your chance to shine, after all!" added Uraraka.

At this, Mineta's frown was replaced by a sheepish smile.

"How about you show me what I can expect from you, my lovely harem dancers? I gotta know what I'm working with, first."

"Sure. Fine. Watch closely, now," said Mina. She

began to dance, and the other girls followed her rhythm. The plan was to put Mineta in the middle, making him the star of this charming routine. The boys cheered in approval of the girls' moves, but the would-be star looked dissatisfied.

"Too tame! You're s'posed to be my *harem*, so try acting like it," he said.

"And how does a harem act, exactly?" asked Asui flatly, with one finger at her lower lip.

"You're s'posed to be in love with me, so how about some wiggly, grinding action! Of course, you'll barely be wearing anything at all during the real thing, so we'll get some skin on skin, y'know? Here, lemme give you a taste of what I'm looking f—"

With ragged breaths and bloodshot eyes, Mineta lunged at Asui in the hope of giving his perverted demonstration, but she caught him with her tongue and slammed him to the ground.

"Talk about looking a gift harem in the mouth!" said Hagakure, whose invisible expression was likely set to "furious." Ashido followed up with a threat.

"Pull that pervy crap again, and we're cutting the harem number altogether! You got that?"

"Suuure, I'll be good. I prooomise," said a sneering Mineta.

"Like we'd ever buy that!" said Uraraka with a snort. Shinso was still observing, at a distance.

He's gotta get expelled for sexual harassment one of these days, right?

With that new concern occupying his head, Shinso finally dropped off the lumber at the trash and headed toward the classroom for the paint. The school building was usually closed on Sundays, but the doors were left unlocked for the duration of this festival prep period.

Shinso heard voices coming from one of the classrooms he was passing, and upon peering through the door's window, he spotted a drum kit, a keyboard, and guitars, along with Katsuki Bakugo, Denki Kaminari, Fumikage Tokoyami, Kyoka Jiro, and Momo Yaoyorozu. They must've been on break, since Yaoyorozu was distributing tea from a thermos.

"Phew, that hits the spot," said Kaminari between slow sips. Meanwhile, Bakugo drained his cup dry in seconds, without a hint of sentimental reflection.

"Tea's tea! Though this one's a little sweeter than yesterday's."

"I should have expected you'd have a distin-guishing palate, Bakugo," said Yaoyorozu. "Today's is a second flush Darjeeling, while yesterday I brought a first flush."

"First? Second? What's the difference?" asked Jiro.

"First flush refers to tea leaves picked during spring, while second means the harvesters waited until summer," said Yaoyorozu as she passed Jiro a cup of tea poured from another thermos. The latter looked confused about why she was the only one getting a different drink, so the former clarified with a smile.

"Yours is milk tea, which should help protect your throat and singing voice. You mentioned some discomfort yesterday, yes?"

"Oh. Thanks… Yeah, this is great," said Jiro.

Seeing Jiro's expression relax, Yaoyorozu finally sat down to enjoy her own cup of tea.

Tokoyami was inspecting some power cords in one corner of the room, but before he could finish, Dark Shadow emerged from his body and shouted.

"Fumikage, gimme something to do!"

"As I explained yesterday, Dark Shadow," said Tokoyami, "the stage will be lit up from all angles. Just the sort of place you cannot tolerate."

"But I'm the only one left out! I wanna do *something*!"

"Aww, why the heck not? We could use a third guitarist!" said Kaminari without second thought. Jiro, on the other hand, wasn't so sure.

"Our whole dynamic would be unbalanced, though. Maybe it could play bass instead?"

"No. That intricate fingering demands extensive practice. Dark Shadow couldn't possibly learn it in time," was Tokoyami's reasoned response.

"I wanna play!" pouted Dark Shadow. "Everyone else gets to join the School Festival!"

With his companion on the verge of tears, Tokoyami was nearing his wit's end.

"Shaddup!" snapped Bakugo. "Wah wah wah! Whining like a baby cuz you wanna play too? Why don'tcha bang on something, then? That's about on your level!"

This gave Jiro an idea.

"Banging... Percussion, maybe? How about the tambourine? It's simple enough, and it could add a nice touch to our arrangement."

"Tambourine... Lemme!" said Dark Shadow.

"In that case, just a moment," said Yaoyorozu,

before producing a fully formed tambourine with her "Creation" Quirk. Dark Shadow snatched the instrument greedily and began jangling away.

"Tch." Bakugo clucked his tongue venomously. "Just don't throw off the damn beat."

"Aye, aye!"

As Shinso finally walked away toward his own classroom, the joyous jangling and Bakugo's roars of "Shaddup!" faded into the distance.

Is it just me, or has Bakugo gotten tamer since the Sports Festival?

Shinso picked up the paint he had come for and walked back down the corridor. The band had resumed practice by the time he passed the other classroom again; he heard them taking the piece from the top over and over. The sounds faded again, and Shinso got to thinking.

Before he'd applied to U.A. High, he never could've imagined putting so much time and effort into anything besides studying on any given Sunday. Surely the training demanded by the Hero Course would occupy every free minute. He hadn't been too far off the mark; U.A.'s classes were as intense as could be and the Hero

Course asked a lot of its students, but the school was also sure to offer a host of laid-back events for the student body's enjoyment, in the name of fostering that standard high school experience for all. Shinso had put U.A. up on a pedestal and overlooked this obvious fact—a fact he was being keenly reminded of through his observations that day.

On his way back to the green, he heard another group of voices around the next corner.

"All right, the clue for this next round is 'white.'"

"Aoyama's probably thinking...'rice'!"

"Wrong. It is 'my skin, that glistens like freshly fallen snow. ☆'"

Shinso held his breath at the sound of one familiar voice in particular and peered around the corner at the source. Bingo—it was Izuku Midoriya.

"Glistening white skin, Aoyama? Only you could come up with an answer like that!"

"Midoriya, if you truly thought my answer would be 'rice,' you were sorely mistaken. Besides which, *pain* is my carbohydrate of choice, ☆" replied Yuga Aoyama. Next to him, Mashirao Ojiro gave an awkward smile.

"Midoriya hasn't been able to guess a single one of your answers yet," he said.

Tenya Ida and Shoto Todoroki were also part of this circle, and this group, too, was apparently taking a break.

The newlywed game? Here? Now?

Shinso wanted to keep moving, but his feet wouldn't budge. Back during the Sports Festival, he'd used his Quirk to manipulate Ojiro. It had seemed like his only path to victory at the time, so he didn't exactly regret his actions, but he'd be lying if he claimed he didn't feel guilty at all.

Then there was Midoriya—the boy who'd defeated him. The one who'd broken the unbreakable hold of the brainwashing and proceeded to beat the struggling Shinso in a contest of strength. An opponent earnest and good natured enough to drop his guard and respond— risking another round of brainwashing—when, after their battle, Shinso vowed to become a hero.

When he'd submitted his transfer request, Shinso had imagined himself one step closer to his dream, but the more he'd trained in the days since, the more anxious he'd grown about the reality looming before him. While the kids of the Hero Course ran on ahead at top speed, here he was, lagging behind. Shinso leaned

against the wall and gripped the paint can even harder.

"How about a more specific, personal topic?" suggested Ida. "For instance...our favorite heroes?"

Everyone besides Midoriya snorted and said, "Too easy," just as Midoriya blurted out, "All Might!"

"If the goal is to get Midoriya and Aoyama in sync, shouldn't they just rehearse?" said Todoroki with all his usual candidness. The others nodded in agreement.

"Be sure to spin my gorgeous self all about so that my sparkles can fill the entire hall! ☆" said Aoyama.

"Sure, I'll do my best!"

I thought class A was just playing some music?

Shinso was no longer sure what sort of spectacle they were planning.

Beyond the wall that divided him from the group, Shinso saw Ida shoot up, inspired by Midoriya's enthusiasm.

"I too have been working on my dance steps! Observe, everyone!"

Choreographer Ashido had decided to make use of Ida's characteristic stiff joints and have him perform a solo robot, which he now demonstrated to the others. His awkward, clunky movements were the spitting image of a mechanized automaton.

"Wow, those are some not-too-smooth moves, Ida! Good going!" said Midoriya.

"Thank you. But I still need to brush up on my routine before the main event," said Ida.

"Hey, why don't you check out the Support Course's robots, for reference?" offered Ojiro. "You're already kind of friends with Mei Hatsume from the Sports Festival, right?"

"No thank you! Unnecessary! I shall find the robot within me without that sort of external aid!" shot back Ida. His first run-in with Hatsume, at the Sports Festival, had turned him into an unwitting walking billboard for her inventions. Later, when he and the others had gone to her for costume upgrades, she'd forced arm boosters on him that had rocketed him straight into the ceiling. Unpleasant memories, to say the least.

Unfazed, Ojiro gave a gentle smile and said, "It's funny how the two festivals couldn't be any more different."

"They call it a sports festival, but it's really just a battle showcase," mused Midoriya. This got Ida reminiscing.

"The obstacle race, the cavalry battle, and then

the orthodox tournament… Ah, come to think of it, everyone here made it to the final sixteen, yes?"

The top sixteen point scorers in the cavalry battle had earned spots in the final tournament, but that particular memory made Ojiro grimace.

"Yeah, though I decided to drop out."

"Oh, right. Because of Shinso…" added Midoriya.

Still eavesdropping, Shinso felt his heart leap into his throat at the sound of his own name.

"Whereas I decided to move on all the same, ☆" said Aoyama with a wink.

While Midoriya seemed to search for the right words, Ojiro gave a frustrated laugh.

"And then—even though I tried to warn you, Midoriya, you let him get you right at the start of your match, with that Brainwashing of his."

Shinso scowled, failing to detect even the faintest note of resentment in Ojiro's voice. He found himself wishing that the tailed boy had hurled some abuse or cursed Shinso's name; then he wouldn't have to feel quite so guilty.

"Yeah, I couldn't help myself…" said Midoriya, returning Ojiro's smile. "I guess I just panicked since, well, the brainwashing was so powerful and…intense. And you don't see mind-control Quirks too often, you know? Imagine being able to stop a villain in their tracks, just like that. But it'd also be super useful for saving people! No matter who you are, it takes time to stop panicking and think clearly—especially when you're in danger and you gotta act fast—so imagine how handy Brainwashing would be for managing a distressed crowd and guiding them to safety… Yeah, I think it's an amazing Quirk!"

Hearing Midoriya divert into muttering-analysis mode, Shinso's whole body clenched up. People had always said his Quirk seemed best suited to a villain, but here was someone else seeing it in the same light he always had. All the comments and jokes about villainous mind control hadn't kept Shinso from admiring heroes, so he'd never stopped believing that his Quirk could actually help people. Midoriya's words filled him with a queasy mix of frustration and joy, and he had to hold back the words trying to escape his own mouth. No—to dash around the corner and say "Thank you!" now would be to rest on laurels he hadn't earned yet. Shinso knew this, deep down. He

knew where his next big step had to take him, and he knew that even *that* was just the real starting point.

Shinso forced a cocksure smile onto his own face and turned around silently, opting for a different, roundabout route. He still had to get stronger before the next time they met.

Beyond the wall, the class A boys kept chatting about the Sports Festival.

"Midoriya versus Todoroki was a battle for the ages, though," said Ojiro.

"Yeah, I really gave it all I had but still came up short!" said Midoriya with a note of frustration in his voice. Hearing this, Todoroki paused for a moment before speaking.

"I might have technically won, but that's not how it felt. Next time, I'm winning for real."

The others stared in mild shock at this declaration, but Todoroki's expression suggested that he might as well have said "The sky is blue"—so obvious was this truth to him. Midoriya realized that they weren't going to get more of an explanation, so he responded in turn.

"Hmph, I wouldn't be so sure! The next victory's gonna be mine!" he said, with fists clenched. Joining the bandwagon, Ida pumped his own fist into the air, up and down.

"You two had better not count *me* out just yet!"

Seeing the trio nodding in solidarity, Ojiro started feeling left out.

"Don't forget about the rest of us, okay? I'm pretty confident in a one-on-one fight."

"And I have been busy perfecting my new moves!" added Aoyama. "Prepare to be blinded by their brilliance! ☆"

The five boys accepted the mutual gauntlet throwing with bold grins on their faces, vowing to keep honing their skills before the next Sports Festival. If they were lucky, it would be on a day as beautiful as this one.

UA

"Making progress?"

"Oh. Aizawa Sensei."

As Shinso took the long way back to his classmates and their patch of grass, he heard Aizawa call out to him.

"We're about halfway done, yeah," he said, realizing

that the can of paint must've reminded Aizawa about class C's haunted house.

"Good to hear," said Aizawa with a light nod. "Keeping up with your training too, I hope?"

Festival organization and frequent hospital visits had been keeping Aizawa busy, so Shinso had been training on his own each day after classes and festival prep.

"Yeah. I know that every second counts at this point."

The curt response was imbued with Shinso's unshakable determination. Sensing this change, Aizawa opened his eyes a little wider than usual and said, "I see," before turning to walk away. Before he could get very far, though, an excited group of students came down the path.

"Mew!"

"Nope, try again! More catlike! Like a little demon!"

"Meowwww!"

"Now I wanna hear that 'stray cat' sound! Cute, yes, but also wild and untamed!"

"Mrrrow!"

"Oh, hey there, Aizawa Sensei!"

The student leading the pack noticed Aizawa, and the rest of the group—wearing cat-ear decorations, clad in literal cat suits, and practicing their honest-to-goodness cat calls—stopped to greet the teacher as well.

"Good meowrning, Sensei!"

"Right. Sure. Carry on."

The cat impersonators moved along, and a dumbfounded Shinso asked, "What on earth was that about?"

"One of the second-year classes is doing a cat cafe where *they're* the cats," explained Aizawa.

So they were honing their cat impressions. An interesting idea, Shinso thought, but going for realism like that only lent them a strange, discomfiting energy.

"Cats are cute *because* they're cats, I say," muttered Shinso under his breath. As a fellow cat person, Aizawa nodded wordlessly.

"I wonder if little girls like cats too…" said Aizawa to himself.

"Little…girls?"

"Fashionwise, I mean."

Aizawa walked away without further explanation.

He's buying clothes for a little girl?

Shinso remembered the paint, tucked away his unanswered questions, and hurried off toward his classmates. This was it—he'd finally decided to tell

them about his transfer application. It wasn't that he'd suddenly grown confident or rid himself of doubts, but announcing one's goals to the world was a good way to cut off one's own escape routes. As Shinso approached his class, however, he noticed that they were on break, chatting excitedly about something or other.

"We oughta do it right after the Sports Festival."

"Yep. Shinso'll be none the wiser if we pretend we're just prepping for the wrap party."

Me? None the wiser about what?

They hadn't noticed him coming back, so Shinso instinctively snuck behind one wall of the haunted house.

"But, man, when d'you think he's gonna tell us about his damn transfer request?"

"It's not like we haven't known for a while now."

"I guess Shinso's just more thoughtful than he lets on."

So they already knew. Shinso found himself blushing and feeling like an idiot for not realizing.

"That's why we're gonna throw him this awesome party—to really light a fire under him!"

"He's the rising star of General Studies, after all."

The eavesdropping Shinso gulped and felt his body clenching up again.

Don't worry, guys—that fire's good and lit now.

With this newfound conviction, he rehearsed his upcoming declaration in his mind.

I'm getting into the Hero Course no matter what, so just watch me.

These classmates of his had also shot for the stars and missed, but here they were, willing to put aside ego and lift him up to those heights. Shinso felt the weight of that implied responsibility, knowing full well how much it would motivate him.

He glanced up at the sky again. Nothing but blue in every direction, but Shinso didn't waste a second wondering where those errant clouds had gone. He turned the corner and said, "I'm back, guys."

Shinso might be saying goodbye to them sooner rather than later, but the warmth he'd found wouldn't be easily left behind.

Part 3

Romeo and Juliet and the Return of the Prisoner King of Azkabum

IT'S A TOTALLY SPECTACULAR ORIGINAL FANTASY SCREENPLAY FROM NONE OTHER THAN CLASS B!!

ROMEO AND JULIET AND THE RETURN OF THE PRISONER KING OF AZKABUM...

"Attention, all—the show is about to begin. Class 1-B proudly presents *Romeo and Juliet and the Return of the Prisoner King of Azkabum*!"

At the sound of the echoing buzzer and announcement, a hush fell over the performance space. The lights dimmed, and the curtain concealing the stage began to rise silently. The darkness and quiet lingered just long enough to get the audience excited before the stage lights slammed on. Class 1-B's play had begun.

"Ahh, what a bracing morning! The sun has awoken from its slumber and now brings light to my beautiful kingdom of Gondur!"

Garbed in an ornate prince costume, Neito Monoma projected his opening lines from a castle balcony. Hearing their cue, Nirengeki Shoda and Yosetsu Awase stepped through a facsimile of a door and appeared behind Monoma.

"Prince Romeo, exposing yourself to the elements in such light garb is just begging to catch cold," said Shoda.

"And when that happens, it'll be us, your retainers, who'll be feeling the king's wrath," added Awase.

Monoma glanced toward the pair, who wore simple shirts and pants befitting their roles as humble retainers.

"My dear Froyo and Samwize. Ha ha ha, worry not about my father and his temper. I will always be here to protect you, so you really needn't scold. Our deep friendship surpasses all notion of class and station, does it not? Why, we three bosom buddies snuck down to a tavern of ill repute for some fun last night!"

"But, Prince Romeo!" said Shoda. "If word of your escapades reaches the wrong ears, our very necks could be on the line!"

"You wanted to see how the lower classes live and, well, you very nearly coerced us into guiding you to town!" said Awase.

"Then we are accomplices. Not merely friends, but partners in crime whose fates are tied to one another. Ha ha ha ha!" said Monoma, his booming laugh earning a few smiles from the audience.

Hidden in the wings off stage left, stage director Juzo Honenuki observed the reaction and sighed in relief.

"Great. Let's keep this up…"

The stage director was responsible for everything surrounding the production. As the one with the most critical behind-the-scenes role, the director had to comprehend every last detail of the play, be aware of each moving cog, and maintain a composed mind-set at all times. Though *Romeo and Juliet and the Return of the Prisoner King of Azkabum* was fundamentally a vehicle for Monoma, its script and planning had been put together by the entire class. Without both the onstage cast and the offstage crew, there would be no play.

Deeper in the wings, the narrow space was filled with additional set pieces, props, and costumes. Watching the stage were the crew members as well as performers waiting for their moment to step out of the shadows.

"But, well, this prince is supposed to be a decent

guy, right? That's how we wrote it, and that's how he's playing it, but when I see Monoma out there, I can't help but think that this character's totally a dirty rotten schemer. Maybe cuz I know him in real life?" said Sen Kaibara, the director's assistant.

"Too true," agreed Kosei Tsuburaba, a stagehand.

"So he ain't holding anything back? Nothing wrong with that!" boomed Tetsutetsu Tetsutetsu at his usual unreasonable volume, despite an earlier warning about backstage etiquette.

"Quiet, Tetsutetsu!" shot back everyone in unison.

"Sorry 'bout that!" said Tetsutetsu just as loudly. He clapped his hands over his own mouth.

"Why don't you wear your mask until it's time to go out there?" suggested Honenuki, hoping that Tetsutetsu might be more inclined to use an indoor voice if his face were covered. The latter was playing the part of Romeo's fated foil, Count Paris, and wasn't due onstage for quite a while.

"No need, dude... What kind of man can't keep quiet when he's told, huh...?" said Tetsutetsu in his loudest possible whisper.

"Please?" begged Honenuki.

Kinoko Komori—who could have easily been mistaken for an actress given her frilly costume and gaudy makeup—gave a bemused laugh.

"Monoma sure was born for the limelight!"

Prop master Shihai Kuroiro stared at Komori from within the darkness of the wing. Instead of speaking up, he clutched an ancient-looking piece of paper and whispered to himself, "Perpetual darkness is my limelight…"

If ever there were someone who fed on attention and shone all the brighter for it, it was Monoma, which is why it raised his hackles whenever class A made headlines without even trying. They were always stealing the proverbial show, and that was something Monoma wouldn't stand for, given his love for his own class B. Glory seekers like Monoma tended to stand tall and unashamed, always performing instinctual mental calculations about how to win over their audience through moving words and stirring actions. In this sense, it was no wonder that Monoma seemed so in his element on the stage.

"Now then, I shall greet my father this morning," said Monoma as he walked off stage left.

"Great start out there," said Honenuki.

"I suppose," said Monoma with a grin before turning to watch Shoda and Awase, whose characters had stayed behind to chat about Romeo.

"Our prince has got some wrinkles to iron out, hasn't he?" said Shoda, as Froyo. "And to think, they're about to send out that royal notice declaring him the official successor to the throne of Gondur!"

"The common folk do feel a kinship with him, what with him being so down to earth, but ruling over the whole kingdom? Sounds like a bit too much, at his age…" said Awase, as Samwize.

"It's a good thing our king is still in good health, I say. In the meantime, he can keep raising Romeo to be a good and decent ruler, so when the time comes…" added Shoda.

From the wings, Monoma watched the pair perform and gave a satisfied nod, as if he were the director himself.

"Good, good. Nirengeki's got the worrywart act nice and polished, and Awase's got down pat that aura of being perpetually flustered," he said.

Honenuki found himself thinking that Shoda's and

Awase's true natures were proving useful to their roles (more so than Monoma's characteristic belligerence toward class A), though he kept this to himself.

Monoma now gave a loud gasp from off stage, portraying Romeo's shock upon learning of the king's disappearance.

"Heh heh, here's the king's letter," said Kuroiro, handing Monoma the prop.

"Thanks."

After a quick glance to confirm that Monoma had the letter in hand, Honenuki turned back to the stage and gave his lead actor a timed cue.

"Father? Oh, Father!" shouted Monoma before bursting back onto the stage with a measured leap.

"Dreadful news... My father...has vanished!"

From stage right, Manga Fukidashi triggered a startling "BAM" sound effect, prompting the three actors to freeze in place. As the one working sound design, it was his job to produce sound effects that accompanied the characters' emotional states and to start and stop the background music with perfect timing.

Director Honenuki had given Fukidashi the cue, and he now told his sound man "Good work" over the wireless comms.

"Would be easier if I could just use my Quirk, but whatever," replied Fukidashi, not actually sounding all that resentful. His Quirk was "Comic," and it allowed him to materialize onomatopoeia in physical form. Of course, an entire play's worth of corporeal sound effects would quickly fill up the stage, so that idea had been scrapped.

"Narration time," said Honenuki, rolling his eyes at Fukidashi's grumbling.

"You got it," said Fukidashi, flipping the switch that fired up Monoma's prerecorded narration track.

"The disappearance of the king of Gondur came like a bolt from the blue."

"Now, Kamakiri," said Honenuki over the comms.

"Right, right," said Togaru Kamakiri, who was working the lights from the wings off stage right, near Fukidashi. The stage lights shut off, and eerie music accompanied Monoma's narration within the darkness.

"With their king gone, the people of Gondur became gripped with unease, and in the capital…"

"We've got forty seconds, people," said Honenuki to cast and crew.

The three actors dashed off stage left for a rapid

costume change, as their characters were about to begin a journey. "Over here, Monoma!" said Komori, and she and others with free hands helped the actors make the quick switch.

Meanwhile, Tsuburaba led the effort to replace the castle set with a forest, assisted by Yui Kodai's "Size," Ibara Shiozaki's "Vines," and Pony Tsunotori's "Horn Cannon." The three girls would be appearing onstage sooner or later, but their Quirks were especially useful for swapping the massive set pieces in the meantime. Honenuki supervised all the work with a stopwatch in hand, periodically updating his classmates on the remaining time. Without a doubt, teamwork was key to this production.

"Ten seconds, nine, eight, seven, six, five, four, three... Annnd, lights."

The lights popped back on to reveal a forest, and in the wings, the scene-change crew celebrated their successful operation with silent thumbs-ups. On Honenuki's cue, Monoma staggered onto the stage.

"Without their king, the people of Gondur suffered. Fearing the complete destruction of his once-beautiful kingdom, Prince Romeo set out in search of his father..."

Just as the narration finished, Monoma reached center stage and collapsed with an anguished cry.

"Where oh where has the king gone...? The father I know and love would never abandon his people, his son, his kingdom! If some foul specter or demon has possessed him, it is my duty to slay this evil and return the king to his throne! Ahh, what tragedy... Or is it comedy? That I, a princeling who neglected his training in the ways of both blade and force must now leave the kingdom for the first time and slay a demon! If only I had studied more under the kingdom's greatest force user, Master Obee-Wun... Indeed, before cursing the tragic nature of my present fate, I would do well to slap my past self for his indolence!"

As Monoma chewed the scenery, the audience found itself more and more captivated by his performance.

As the plot would have it, Romeo would leave in search of the king; encounter his destined love, Juliet; do some growing as a person; battle his fated enemy, Count Paris; learn a shocking truth; and become a fine monarch in his own right. The character names all sounded awfully familiar, but Monoma had insisted that any resemblance to existing intellectual properties was entirely coincidental. It was a hodgepodge of a story, filled with adventure, drama, romance, and revenge, all stewed together into a tasty tale. Itsuka Kendo's participation in the festival's beauty pageant had kept her from joining the play, but she and Reiko Yanagi (her pageant attendant) had watched the dress rehearsal and been moved by the stirring plot. If it could have that effect on those who knew Monoma's off-kilter personality all too well, then surely it would resonate with an audience that was none the wiser. Yes, class B was aiming to put on a production that would earn a standing ovation and then some.

"If that's how you're feeling, then come on back to Gondur with us!" said Awase, as Samwize, as he and Shoda dashed onto the stage in pursuit of Monoma's Romeo.

"Froyo! Samwize! Why are you here?"

"Master Obee-Wun's out there looking for his majesty as well," said Shoda, as Froyo. "We bumped into him, and he asked us to pass you a message."

"That's right—he says, 'Beware Count Paris.' You got any idea who that might be, Prince Romeo?" said Awase.

"Count Paris... I met the man at a banquet once,

but…why would Master Obee-Wun give me such a warning…?" said Monoma, seeming lost.

"Also," said Shoda, pulling a golden ring from his pocket, "he wants you to have this—the legendary ring passed down through the royal family for generations…"

"Said something about that ring protecting those of the royal bloodline… Sorta like a guardian talisman, we're thinking?" suggested Awase.

Monoma shook his head.

"I…never knew about such a ring," he said, looking perplexed.

"We're told it's given to princes when they ascend the throne," said Shoda.

"Why, this precious ring is beautiful enough to bewitch my very soul…" said Monoma, taking the ring in hand and lifting it high, telling the audience it was sure to be a key plot point going forward.

Shiozaki watched from the wings, clasped her hands in prayer, and began muttering, "I am the spirit of the ring… I *am* the spirit of the ring…" She wasn't due onstage just yet, but she felt the need to psych herself up for the role.

"Relaaax, you'll be great," said Kaibara, trying to

soothe his stressed classmate. "You already come off as pretty darn spiritual in everyday life, Shiozaki."

"Thank you, but I am not concerned with the appearance of the character so much as her psychology... Should this spirit have a merciful heart befitting a servant of the Lord, or be more of a nature sprite, prone to whimsy?"

Behind Shiozaki, Tsunotori and Jurota Shishida were changing into furry, beast-like costumes.

"You will do very good in this role, I think. The three of us practiced a lot!" said Tsunotori.

"Remember all those early mornings, Shiozaki?" added Shishida. "When you went into the woods and prayed to the spirits of nature? And how the two of us ran around the woods all free and wild, to get into the mind-set of the hippogriffs who serve the ring spirit?"

"Oh? That explains the rumors about the weird growls coming from the woods," said Tsuburaba, who'd been listening.

"People heard us, really?" said Shishida.

"We are very sorry about that!" said Tsunotori.

"Stand by for you-know-what," said Honenuki, turning around to the group.

"Ohh, the big surprise!" said Tsunotori.

"I am reluctant to startle these good people who have done us the honor of attending our performance..." said Shiozaki.

"A good shocker is part of what makes a show, a show," insisted Shishida, as he and Tsunotori led the less-than-enthusiastic Shiozaki behind the set. Setsuna Tokage, Kuroiro, Tsuburaba, and Hiryu Rin took deep, excited breaths and followed them out.

"Make it happen, guys," said Honenuki.

"I'll prove I'm worthy of the *dragon* kanji in my name," said Rin with a grin before disappearing down the passageway.

"Bring down the house, dudes..." cheered Tetsutetsu in that same whisper-shout.

After seeing his stagehands off, Honenuki turned to Kodai, who was receiving finishing touches on her makeup from Komori.

"You're almost up, Kodai."

"Mhm," replied Kodai.

"Our leading lady looks ready for action!" said Tetsutetsu.

"Ooh, totally..." added Kojiro Bondo.

Hearing the boys' compliments, Komori (the costumer and makeup artist) puffed out her chest and gave a haughty chuckle. Kodai's simple one-piece dress accentuated her refined features, and though her typical lack of expressiveness stood out, it would lend her character an air of mystery. In fact, she'd been chosen for the role for just that reason; any emoting she did do would be all the more striking. Kodai was the type who could draw attention even without putting on a big show, so they hadn't written too many lines into the script for the taciturn girl.

"Ahh, this hunger pains me so…" moaned Monoma, as Romeo. "Meat… I must sate the carnivore within… I cannot take another step otherwise…"

"But, my prince, there're rumors of monsters in these woods… We won't be finding any ordinary rabbits for dinner, I reckon," said Awase.

"Wait just a second… Here we are!" said Shoda. "I stashed away some jerky in my bag, just for emergencies!"

"Give it here, friend! Your prince commands you!"

"Sheesh… Some prince you're turning out to be!"

"Silence! Prince or not, would you deny a starving man a meal?"

"Why, I never thought I'd see you turn your blade on us, Romeo!"

"You were grumbling earlier about how you're not fit to be a prince, so c'mon, then... We'll cross swords as equals, and the winner will claim the jerky as his prize!"

"Rahhh!"

And thus did a desperate sword fight unfold upon the stage, pitting friend against friends in a life-or-death struggle. On the surface, it revealed how raw, ugly hunger can transform a person, and yet the sublime scene posed questions about the very dignity of man. Sound effects and flashes of light accompanied the clashing blades, and the audience watched with bated breath. The prince lost the battle in the end, but his friends shared the jerky anyway, leading to tears and renewed comradery.

"Oh... What exquisite morsels of dried meat... Even the delicacies of Gondur—grilled spring breeze robin and rare gator hangnail steak—cannot compare! Friends, won't you forgive me for my foolishness?" said Monoma.

"We won't," replied Shoda.

"Huh?"

"Not unless you swear to be a great king in your own right."

"Ah, of course—I swear, here and now, that as king of Gondur, I will ensure that our people will never again know hunger, nor misfortune!"

Seeing the young prince set his eyes upon a bright future, the audience burst into a round of applause. Shoda noticed the smug grin rising on Monoma's face and did some quick ad-libbing to move things along.

"Come, my prince! The journey continues!" he said, tugging Monoma's arm to lead him down the faux forest path.

"Are you trying to ruin my big moment?" hissed Monoma, turning his back to the audience for a moment.

"You've got the audience squarely on your side," whispered back Shoda. "But that won't last if they see the prince smirking and soaking up the glory."

"Nice improvising, Nirengeki," said Awase, also whispering.

Monoma looked ready to resist for a second, but he turned his frown around and said, "Well, now it's time for our fair Juliet's debut."

An instant later, Kodai, as Juliet, emerged atop a massive, craggy boulder.

"Somebody, help me!" she cried, just as an enormous dragon popped out behind her. Screams rose from the audience when it barreled forward to the first row of seating, illuminated by just enough stage lights to seem terrifyingly real.

"I've got you!" shouted Monoma as Kodai leaped from the crag into his waiting arms.

"Dragon!" screamed Shoda.

"Time to run!" said Awase. "This way!" he added, as the two retainers helped Monoma and Kodai to their feet.

Just as the actors started to run, the lights blacked out, and when they flashed on again, the dragon was flying across the performance space. Before the audience could stop screaming, the lights flickered again, and this time the dragon was soaring from the back of the room. Then, directly above the audience. Shiozaki and the others with Quirks suited to manipulating the dragon puppet kept repositioning it in time with the brief blackouts, and with each pass, some of the scales from Rin's Quirk scattered down from above, further upping the realism.

The unceasing cries were a blend of wonder and excitement that earned a satisfied nod from Honenuki

behind the scenes. He was glad that the audience found the whole thing delightful, but it was his job to keep the show moving along. The relatively pleased stage director spoke into his wireless mic, giving the next cue.

"Lightning in six, five, four, three..."

The stage lighting simulated a flashing thunderbolt, and the dragon's roars seemed to fade into the distance. The drip-drop sound of water falling echoed through-out the now-silent auditorium, and a dim spotlight shone upon one corner of the stage, highlighting Romeo and Juliet, who had gotten separated from Froyo and Samwize during the chase.

"Thank you for saving me," said Kodai.

"Your thanks are unnecessary... My name is Romeo. Tell me, maiden, why was that dragon after you to begin with?" said Monoma.

A pause. Kodai said nothing.

"You do not wish to say? Very well. But if nothing else, tell me your name."

"Juliet."

"I rejoice upon hearing it, for now I am no longer ignorant of the name given to this world's most beautiful creature..."

Watching the pair stare into each other's eyes, Tetsutetsu couldn't hold back.

"That's our Monoma... Managing that embarrassing, sappy line with a straight face..."

"I love a good romance!" said Komori, blushing something fierce, just as the dragon-wrangling crew crept back into the wings. Meanwhile, onstage, Monoma's Romeo came to a sudden realization.

"Juliet...? Why, you couldn't be Princess Juliet of the Kingdom of Rowhan, longtime enemy to my fair Gondur...? Please, Juliet, say it is not so...?"

Kodai nodded curtly, and Monoma's shock was accompanied by a bit of tragic background music and a sharp spotlight that tracked him as he staggered to center stage.

"Juliet... Oh, Juliet, Juliet... Wherefore art thou Juliet! Have the gods no mercy in their hearts, to make the rival princess my first love? I curse you, foul gods! Do you delight in rending my heart to shreds? Damnable gods! Would you see all the lovers of this world thrown into hell? Go on, burn the very notion of love to cinders! Ha ha ha ha ha! Ahh ha ha ha!"

The audience gulped, startled by Monoma's ghastly monologue.

"Monoma was born to play these sorts of tragic, flawed characters, yeah?" said an impressed Tokage.

"Tragic, flawed characters? Well yeah—cuz he's already one of those to start with," quipped Rin, as Monoma's mad peal of laughter brought a chill over the room.

Kodai stood slowly, gripped Monoma's hand, and stared at him.

"No. It mustn't burn," she said.

These words seemed to quell the boy's raging heart, and the audience was smitten.

"Indeed I was ignorant, but I know now there are no gods in this world—only angels..." he said, almost reverent. Monoma continued, now whispering softly to Kodai.

"Your eyes are as glimmering treasures, concealed eons prior within the dark pool of a cave. Your cold beauty shines as does lapis lazuli, poised to steal my heart! Your raven hair, smooth as silk... Why, I find myself fearing it may meld into the darkness that envelops us and vanish from this earthly plane. Your ivory cheek invites my caressing hand, though I suspect I may then never have use of that hand again..."

Kodai stared wordlessly.

"No, I understand. It would not do to have my hand stuck fast to your cheek for the rest of our days... And yet, I wish that you could know how my heart now throbs! Would that I could pluck it from my chest, such that you might hear its cries and know as I do that we are each other's destiny! I would lay down my very life if doing so could prove my love for you, Juliet! You may be the princess of the people I call enemy, but now, I would..."

The ring fell from Monoma's pocket at that moment, and he gasped.

"Ah! But I am sworn to another quest! I must track down the king! How can I possibly choose? Wait. I deceive myself in speaking of choice, when there is in fact no cause to set either duty aside! Juliet, though I may seem to you a road-weary wanderer, I shall be a fine king someday, and I vow upon all that is good to mend the relations between our lands. Yes, we shall be husband and wife, leading our people into an era of peace and prosperity! Won't you be my future queen...?"

After an unbearably long pause, Kodai nodded.

"My precious one... My love for you, I swear upon this ring..." said Monoma, embracing Kodai.

Spellbound sighs rose from the girls in the audience, while the jealous boys grumbled. In the wings, Komori and Tsunotori went, "Aww," while Kaibara glanced at Kodai's expression and gave a wry smile.

"Would it kill Kodai to look a little more enthusiastic about this development?" he said.

"Hey, Yui's doing her best out there," said Tokage, in Kodai's defense.

Still watching the stage and without turning around, Honenuki spoke.

"No, it's fine. Her blank expression will make the audience think she's a girl grappling with internal conflict, just like Monoma suggested."

All eyes in the room were on Kodai and her lack of emotion. Yes, Monoma was more than willing to sacrifice the limelight for a moment if it meant making his beloved class B's production a success. Despite his questionable personality, he had gotten into U.A. High, which was proof enough of his talent and dedication.

Shoda and Awase ran up to the pair, reuniting the group at last, but the dazed look on Romeo's face put their characters ill at ease.

"Just about time for me to make some trouble..."

said Tetsutetsu, donning a cloak and stepping toward Honenuki. "This lovey-dovey moment is about to get wrecked!"

"Make the audience hate your guts, man!" said Kaibara.

The other backstage boys cheered on Tetsutetsu too, and on Honenuki's cue, he dashed out onto the stage, snatched up Kodai like a sudden gale, took a deep breath, and began to shout.

"I'll be taking back *what's mine* now!"

The audience was dumbfounded by the appearance of the unknown character now yelling in their faces, and so were Tetsutetsu's classmates in the wings. Honenuki planted his face in his palm and shook his head. This character's debut scene was meant to be silent and ominous, but Tetsutetsu's frustration over

having to keep his voice down the whole time had finally boiled over and been unleashed.

"Who is this, now? Prince Romeo of Gondur?" he roared.

"It's you, Count Paris! But why? How...? Give me back my Juliet!" shot back Monoma, before

turning his back to the audience and switching to a furious whisper.

"What're you supposed to be? You sound like the local shopkeeper who's caught a kid shoplifting! Dial it back!"

Taking the criticism to heart, Tetsutetsu made an expression that seemed to say "Oh, crap!" and then switched to the grimmest face he could muster.

"We will meet again..." he said as quietly as he'd been in the wings, having overcorrected.

Murmurs of "Huh? What'd he say?" rose from the audience, and Tetsutetsu's classmates offstage all hung their heads. Honenuki calmly glanced up at the catwalk above the stage and gave the waiting Shishida a cue. With Kodai under one arm, Tetsutetsu used his other hand to grab a dangling rope all but invisible to the audience. As he rose into the air, Monoma shouted, "We'll meet again? What on earth does that mean...? Nooo, Juliet!"

"Sorry, guys..." said a gloomy Tetsutetsu, back in the wings.

"Don't sweat it!"

"You'll get the volume right next time!"

Onstage, Romeo—who wanted to pursue Juliet— was at odds with Froyo and Samwize, who thought that searching for the king took precedent.

"Did Master Obee-Wun ever speak of her? And why would Count Paris kidnap fair Juliet...? No, this is no time for arguing—I must rescue her!"

"We know how you feel, Prince Romeo!" said Shoda. "But as our prince, your main duty is to find his majesty the king."

"You know how I feel? How could you know! I may be a prince, but first and foremost I am a man! One who can ill abandon the woman he loves! Once Juliet is back by my side, our quest will resume... I do not ask you to understand, no... Farewell! I must walk this path alone!"

With that, Monoma dashed off stage right, and the retainers cried "Prince Romeo!" in unison. Shoda then

heard a strange commotion from stage left, but he quickly regained his focus.

"Thus did Prince Romeo chase after his beloved Juliet..." came Monoma's narration.

Shoda and Awase ran off stage left and breathed satisfied sighs of relief, knowing that their characters

wouldn't show up again until the climax of the show.

"This is unusable..." said a flustered Honenuki. The two actors moved toward the chattering backstage group to find out what had happened. Kuroiro held a white clod of something or other with silver fragments poking out here and there.

"What's that?" asked Awase.

"It's what's left of one of our prop swords..." explained Kaibara.

An upcoming scene would feature space warrior Rei (played by Tokage) and her spacetrooper (played by Rin), who were supposed to be wielding saber blades. When one of the swords had broken backstage, Bondo had offered to use his "Cemedine" Quirk to repair it, but a sudden sneeze on his part had ended up discharging more glue than planned. When Tetsutetsu had rushed over to help, he'd gotten tripped up by a gluey glob on the floor, had activated his "Steel" Quirk on instinct, and had fallen directly onto the already broken sword, crushing it further. The others had done their best to repair it, but the former sword now resembled an avant-garde sculpture. If Bakugo, Kirishima, or Kaminari had been present, they might've been reminded of Shiketsu High's

Seiji Shishikura, whose odd Quirk could turn people into misshapen meatballs. Unlike Shishikura's meatballs, though, this ball of glue and silver would never be whole again, and they had no replacement on hand.

"What now?" said Tokage in a panic. "Can we manage without it...?"

"The saber battle has to happen. We'll just find something that can substitute for the sword," said the ever-composed Honenuki.

"You got it," said Kaibara, racing off with Kuroiro.

There were spare swords attached to Shoda's and Awase's hips, but everyone was too flustered to notice. They could hardly be blamed, as this was class B's first stage production.

"Juliet...? Wherefore hast thou been kidnapped, my Juliet?"

Just as Monoma was starting to wonder why Tokage and Rin hadn't shown up on cue, he caught a glimpse of Honenuki in the wings, making a gesture that implied, "Vamp, and buy us some time."

What could've happened back there...? Well, I'll do what I can.

"Oh, Juliet..." said Monoma, ad-libbing. "Merely

speaking your name fills me with the strength to go on. I've eaten nary a thing for three days and nights, but your name alone sates my hunger… My love for you nourishes and gives me life. I've no need for the many culinary specialties of Gondur, such as sugared potahto-potato with tomato-tomahto jelly, or apeeling river banana wraps, or shorthorn beef with sauce from between a goblin's teeth, or stewed weasel served on an easel, or softshell turtle stuffed in giant tortoise turducken, or japing jaguar cutlets over jasmine rice, or the horns of one-and-a-half long-eared giraffes, or lion tail deep-fried in mane grease, or cookies shaped like a baby elephant's kneecaps, or midnight pasta with inky splats from a black-hearted bat, or even sluggish, short-lived werebunny soup. Yes, love alone is enough for me…"

Did that buy them enough time?

Another gesture from Honenuki, apologetically begging for a few more moments.

Without so much as a hint that he was going off script, Monoma continued with the ad-libbing.

"My Juliet, your Kingdom of Rowhan prefers seafood, yes? Your large subterranean lake delivers all manner of aquatic delicacies to your plate, such as crusty crustacean corn cakes, which they say leave the lucky diner grinning for days on end. Why, just imagining such a dish brings a smile to my weary face. Have you ever partaken, Juliet? We ought to share those crusty cakes and enjoy a lifetime of smiles... Ah, Rowhan is also known for the tuna triple-down, yes? Three helpings of white rice, sandwiched between three whole fish, said to extend one's life for three years if eaten in utter solitude over the course of three days. A dish I would feed my father, if given the chance..."

Hmm? Gosh, finally... What took them so long?

Monoma caught the "okay" gesture from Honenuki and went over the next scene in his mind.

So Tokage and Rin are about to show up as the space-faring survivors of the Rebellious Alliance...

As Romeo, he looked up and gasped.

"W-what manner of craft is that?" he screamed.

A metallic humming sound accompanied a UFO in the process of crash-landing. Monoma's Romeo approached in trepidation, and the spaceship door burst open to reveal Tokage and Rin.

"Are you okay, Rei?" asked Rin, dressed like a space soldier.

Tokage, as Rei, said "Yeah…" but flinched at the sight of Monoma. "Damn… This scout beat us here! How far will the Star Empire go to mess with us…?"

"Die, imperial dog!" shouted Rin.

"Wait! I haven't the faintest idea who you are," shot back Monoma.

They were coming up on another sword fight—a key scene that would show how much Prince Romeo had grown since his stunning loss at the Battle of Jerky. This was a fight they'd rehearsed over and over, and the final product was sure to show the fruits of their efforts.

"Shut your mouth!" said Tokage. "Long live space democracy!"

Tokage comes at me first, then Rin with an immediate follow-up. I dodge them both by a hair's breadth and… Hmm?

Monoma spotted the weapons that Tokage and Rin had pulled from behind their backs with gusto.

"Why baseball bats?" he said, forgetting he was onstage for a moment.

Surely enough, they were wielding a pair of metal baseball bats as if they were swords. The audience members close enough to see had some confused comments as well, which helped Monoma snap back into character. He spotted another gesture from Honenuki—a combination of "Sorry" and "Go on, go on." Apparently, Kuroiro and Kaibara had borrowed the replacement weapons from a class that was running batting cages during the festival.

"One of the swords broke. We had no choice!" hissed Tokage.

"We just gotta make do," whispered Rin.

"No choice, I suppose!" replied Monoma, bracing himself and shifting into a battle stance.

As the trio traded blows, Monoma pretended to be beaten back.

"What fearsome blades, unlike any known to these lands! Are these the renowned saber blades?"

The bat-wielding duo might've come off like a couple of downtown street punks, but Monoma's quick, improvised exposition transformed them back into members of the Rebellious Alliance, equipped with high-tech swords that just happened to resemble earthly baseball bats. Off on stage right, Fukidashi ramped up the action-packed sound effects, and Kamakiri did his best to dazzle the audience with flashing lights.

"I think the audience bought it," said Honenuki.

The rest of the panicked backstage crew felt some of the tension leave the air.

"Thank God for Monoma..." said Kaibara.

"Monoma... We should have a midnight banquet in honor of your courage," added Kuroiro, though neither boy would've uttered these words of appreciation to Monoma's face.

To the classmates in the wings, the sword fight onstage started to take on an air of desperation, but for the audience, this only translated as fierce intensity.

"Kuroiro, do you happen to know where the ring is?" asked Shiozaki.

"Huh? The big one? It should be right over here," said Kuroiro, walking to a table covered in props. Failing to find the ring in question, he said, "I swear it was just here..." Honenuki and the others noticed and asked what was wrong.

"The ring we're about to use—I left it on this table, but now it's gone..." explained Kuroiro.

Shiozaki's scene was coming up (with her as the spirit of the ring), and they had prepared a scaled-up version of Monoma's golden ring, big enough for the audience to see. It was nearly time, but nobody could find it. Unbeknownst to them, during the earlier commotion over the broken sword, the ring had fallen from the table and rolled between the floorboards down into a storage room. Unfortunately, they wouldn't find it until cleanup, long after the play had ended.

"Oh dear. The Lord has presented us with a trial to overcome," said Shiozaki, hands clasped in fervent prayer. Even Shishida and Tsunotori were looking anxious.

"Ugh, not again! What's our move this time?" said Kaibara, glancing at Honenuki. The director thought for a moment before speaking.

"We'll need to find a replacement. Or make one…"

There was no time to run off to other stalls or events.

"Right. So, we need something round, with a hole in the middle!" said Kaibara, frantically looking around. Just as the others joined the search, Tetsutetsu said, "How about this…?"

He held up a dimpled, tube-shaped, lightly grilled snack made of processed fish paste. Tetsutetsu had packed this piece of *chikuwa* that morning in case he got hungry during the production.

"That'll do," said Kuroiro, grabbing the chikuwa and chopping off a slice with his box cutter.

"See?"

The others nodded in agreement.

"Wait, I've got some gold eyeshadow," said Komori.

"Oh… Thanks," said Kuroiro, taking the makeup and brushing it onto the slice of fish paste until it resembled an actual ring, albeit one with personality and a bit of an odor.

"This is really gonna work!" said Kaibara, giving Shiozaki a thumbs-up. But as she received the replacement ring from Kuroiro, Shiozaki looked as if she'd just been sentenced to death by crucifixion.

"Now I suppose I am the spirit of the processed fish snack…"

Her pale expression seemed to ask how to get in the chikuwa mind-set, so Tsunotori and Shishida stepped in with some advice.

"Maybe you are in very much pain, from being box cutted? Or from the grilling process?" suggested Tsunotori.

"Or maybe you're the spirit of the fish that died to make this chikuwa?" offered Shishida.

Shiozaki looked even more aghast now, so Honenuki calmly intervened.

"It's not *really* chikuwa. Just a ring that sort of resembles chikuwa."

Back on the stage, the sword fight had ended, and Romeo was hashing out the misunderstanding with the pair from the Rebellious Alliance.

"I believe with all my heart that you people will liberate the galaxy far, far, far away! Perhaps my own kingdom will achieve space travel one day? On that occasion, Rei, I hope you will come when Gondur calls for aid!" said Monoma's Romeo.

"Of course, Romeo. We'll fight to bring everlasting peace to the galaxy!" said Tokage, as Rei.

"We'd better blast off, Rei," said Rin, as the spacetrooper.

"You'll survive this," said Tokage. "Until we meet again."

"It is a promise, then. And on that day, I shall treat you to another of Gondur's specialties—steamed tanuki undercarriage hot pot!"

Tokage followed Rin back into the UFO and waved back to Monoma.

"Ha ha ha, you bet. I'd love to meet this Juliet of

yours, too... Oh, by the way—we spotted something during our crash landing."

"Oh? What was it?"

"An ominous castle, just a bit north from here. It looked like a creepy man was arguing with a girl about something..."

"I daresay you caught sight of Count Paris and my Juliet..."

"Rei! No time to lose!" said Rin.

"On that note, Romeo, may the force be within you," said Tokage as the door closed and the UFO rose up and out of sight. Monoma ambled toward center stage and began his next monologue.

"So Juliet awaits me to the north... But who is this Count Paris, really? He claimed that she belonged to him, so I suppose she ran from him to begin with? Was she betrothed to him, I wonder...? No! Juliet promised me her hand in marriage! Her heart lies with me! That said, it would be no great surprise to learn that she had been offered to some other royal, to strengthen ties with a foreign kingdom. Is Paris in fact a king, and Juliet's future bridegroom? How terrible that would be! What am I to do, should that prove to be the case?"

As the lovestruck Romeo writhed in anguish and collapsed in despair, a beam of light shot down from above.

"Romeo... Romeo..." echoed Shiozaki's voice.

"Who calls to me?" said Monoma with a start.

"Romeo... I rest inside your pocket..."

Before Monoma could take the ring fully from his pocket, the stage lights flashed and temporarily blinded the audience. In that moment, the golden chikuwa descended from above on a string, so that it would seem to be floating once the audience's eyes adjusted to the light.

As the spirit of the ring, Shiozaki came riding in atop her hippogriffs (Tsunotori and Shishida), whose roars added to the divine mystique of the scene and earned a "Whoaaa" from the audience. But Monoma sniffed the air, realized the stench was coming from the prop ring, and furrowed his brow.

"I am definitely not the spirit of the chikuwa... Rather, the spirit of that original ring. No matter what anyone tells you."

The awkward ad-libbing from Shiozaki cleared up the mystery for Monoma.

Why chikuwa?

Monoma twitched, employing all of his willpower to keep from quipping back loudly. Instead, he pretended to be shocked by the appearance of the ring spirit.

"The spirit of the ring, you say...?"

"Listen well, Romeo... I am always with you...and when your heart desires it, I will come to your aid... And one last time: I am *not* the spirit of the chikuwa..."

With that reminder, the hippogriffs roared again and bore the spirit of the ring up and out of sight. Audience members began to question "Why chikuwa?" too, but Monoma acted fast to distract them.

"What providence! That was very clearly the spirit of the ring... The very ring passed down through my royal family for generations!"

He gasped.

"I mustn't dillydally—Juliet awaits me!" he said, gazing at an imagined horizon with a look of determination. The audience had been placated, and the crew in the wings breathed yet another sigh of relief. Shiozaki, Tsunotori, and Shishida were also glad to be done with their big scene.

"That guy sure can get it done..." said Tetsutetsu with a mouth half-full of chikuwa—a little snack before his next scene. The show was nearing its climax, and the excitement backstage was palpable. In the coming minutes, Count Paris would slay Master Obee-Wun and declare himself Romeo's father before their final showdown outside Paris's castle.

"Lights are down soon, people," said Honeuki. "Stand by for the final set change."

Everyone was poised and ready to go.

"Six, five, four, three… All right, we've got fifty seconds to do this."

Honenuki's new countdown began, and they sprang into action. Monoma pitched in too, and as he did, he asked Kaibara to clarify a few things.

"Why the baseball bats and chikuwa?"

"Things happen. I'll explain once the show's done."

"Fine. Oh, one thing—about that chikuwa used for the ring…"

But they had less than ten seconds left, so Kaibara snapped back, "I said later, man. Good luck," before running offstage again.

"But the smell…" said Monoma, cut off by the stage lights that forced him to transform back into Romeo.

"I've arrived at last… Surely this is the castle Rei

espied from the air...?" muttered Monoma, gazing up at a facsimile of an eerie stone castle. With this last set change completed, the backstage crew members were already in a celebratory mood, along with the actors who'd finished their final scenes. Despite this, Honenuki maintained his composure and prepared to give his final cues.

"We've still got the midair battle. Stand by, everyone," he said, prompting the crew to scurry off to their posts.

"Counting on you guys..." muttered an uncharacteristically nervous Tetsutetsu in an unusually low voice.

"It went fine during rehearsal, so don't worry," said Honenuki. "Get out there and give it your all, but not quite at max volume, okay?"

"Mm-hmm," added Kodai with a reassuring nod.

"Yeah, I'll nail it just right this time..." said Tetsutetsu, nodding back.

On Honenuki's cue, Tetsutetsu strode out onto the stage. Remembering Monoma's tips during rehearsal, he paused just long enough to draw the audience in before speaking in a low, gravelly tone.

"What's this? An uninvited guest who still shows up late? You kept me waiting, Prince Romeo."

Great. That's perfect.

Monoma gave a small smile and a nod at Tetsutetsu's performance before slipping back into his own role.

"I should have known you were the 'creepy man,' Count Paris! Where is Juliet?"

"I'm free to do whatever I so choose with my property, boy…"

"You refuse to release her…? Then I will reclaim my love by force! Arrrgh!"

Monoma lunged at Tetsutetsu, but a swift kick from the villainous Count Paris sent brave Romeo tumbling backward.

"This man is no slouch!" said Monoma, putting on his best shocked face.

"Stand back, Romeo—I shall engage this one in battle," came a voice from behind.

"It's you…Master Obee-Wun!"

Obee-Wun (played by Bondo) had shown up on the scene with Froyo and Samwize in tow.

"Obee-Wun appeared before us during our search for the king," explained Shoda. "There's something you really need to know, Prince Romeo!"

"Romeo," said Bondo, "you've always been negligent

of your studies of the force, and none would call you an exemplary apprentice, but you've been something of a grandson to me since the day you were born... That is why I must be the one to defeat Paris..."

"Yours is a face I've not seen in ages, Obee-Wun... But you will not be rejoicing at this little reunion when I send you to your doom," said Tetsutetsu. His sharp glare and composed voice gave him a larger-than-life presence. Backstage, the rest of the class was impressed by the performances.

"Our little Tetsutetsu is really doing it!" said Tsuburaba, nodding wildly.

"What're you, his mother?" quipped Kaibara.

In the face of Tetsutetsu's overwhelmingly villainous aura, the audience hung on every word with bated breath.

"This man is a phantom, once imprisoned in Azkabum... A specter no longer fit for this world..." said Bondo.

In the wings, Kuroiro shuddered at this dark and broody line from Obee-Wun.

"The infamous prison, Azkabum? What crime did Paris commit to find himself there?" shouted Monoma.

"It was in Azkabum that I left this mortal coil and was reborn. Brought back to do what I must," said Tetsutetsu.

"Not another foul word from those wicked lips, phantom... Hahh!"

Bondo charged at Tetsutetsu, and his force attack sent the latter flying backward.

"You powers have not grown weak, old man," said Tetsutetsu as he floated into the air.

"Master Obee-Wun!" shouted Monoma.

"Leave this fight to me, you three..." said Bondo, who also began to rise.

The midair force battle that ensued was made possible by Tsunotori's "Horn Cannon," Tokage's "Lizard Tail Splitter," and Rin's "Scales," which supported the two battler's bodies so they could clash in the space above the stage. As they traded force blows, Bondo and Tetsutetsu shifted their fight to the open part of the auditorium, directly over the audience. Kaibara set off firecrackers he'd attached to the walls in advance, adding to the spectacle and keeping the audience's eyes glued to the midair scene. The fighters paused, and Tetsutetsu's cold stare and chilling words silenced the riled audience.

"Obee-Wun, you may not have changed, but I certainly have… The power I have attained is like none you've ever held!"

Tetsutetsu's Paris then dealt a finishing blow to Bondo's Obee-Wun, who crashed onto the stage.

"Master Obee-Wun!" cried Monoma, running to the fallen warrior.

"But how…?" questioned Shoda. "He's the mightiest in all of Gondur…"

"Romeo… You mustn't let that man near our kingdom… Listen well… You must be the one to ascend the throne…" said Bondo. He gave one last shudder and was still.

"No… No, Obee-Wun… I had so much yet to learn from you…" said Monoma, weeping and cradling his fallen master.

"Prince Romeo… No, *just* Romeo…" said Tetsutetsu, approaching slowly.

"Romeo!" shouted Shoda and Awase, causing Monoma to spin around and gasp.

"Juliet!" he cried, spotting Kodai on the castle's terrace. Behind her, the roaring dragon perched on the castle tower and glared at the Gondurian trio. Romeo dried his eyes and stood, prepared to face Count Paris at last.

"My name is Romeo! Now hear me, Count Paris, phantom of Azkabum! I shall be taking back my Juliet!"

Tetsutetsu's face transformed, making Paris look almost regretful.

"But, Romeo... What Obee-Wun told you about your father... That he was the king of Gondur... That was a lie."

Tetsutetsu paused and flung back his costume's hood.

"I am your father!"

"Nooooo!" cried Monoma. Violent flashes of light and crashing sound effects accompanied the scream, representing the turmoil in Romeo's heart. The audience was also dumbfounded by this third act twist.

"Now, call me Daddy!"

"Nooo! That's impossible! You, my father? It cannot be! Besides which, my father yet lives! He departed from our kingdom, but I now search for him!"

"Is that the lie Obee-Wun fed you? No, your true father is..."

"I'll have no more of your falsehoods! Juliet, I am here for you!" shouted Monoma, charging at Tetsutetsu with blade in hand.

"Wait. Tetsutetsu's acting funny," said Kaibara,

over in the wings. Count Paris was supposed to dodge Romeo's attack gracefully, but Tetsutetsu seemed to be clutching his stomach in pain. Monoma took notice and flinched backward.

"He's looking green around the gills... Is he sick?" wondered Honenuki with a note of concern in his voice.

"Ack, maybe it was this?" said a panicked Tokage, offering the plastic wrapper from the chikuwa and pointing to a long-since-passed expiration date. The backstage crew whipped their heads back toward Tetsutetsu, who was now practically writhing in pain. Monoma had tried to tell them about the awful stench earlier, but he'd gone ignored.

"Ugh! Why didn't that idiot check the date, shroom!" said Komori, halfway between concerned and furious. While Kuroiro attempted to soothe her, Honenuki fell deep into thought.

"In any case," he said calmly, "we need to get Tetsutetsu off the stage. The show can't continue like this."

The crew glanced back at Tetsutetsu and raised no objections. But how to go about it?

"How can we move on from this scene without Tetsutetsu? That's the question... Monoma could carry it alone, maybe... But Tetsutetsu might be out for good, depending. In that case, we might have to..."

Going off script and ending the show with some ad-libbing seemed like the inevitable solution, but even that was easier said than done. With this weighty decision before them, the members of class B stared at each other, feeling lost.

"Instead of limping to the finish line with some half-assed improvisation, we could always just end the show right here?" suggested Rin, but Honenuki shook his head.

"The show must go on. Once the curtain rises, it cannot fall until the fat lady sings. The audience out there came today to see what we put together, so we owe them that much, at least. Our pride is on the line."

The others looked impressed by Honenuki's valiant take on showmanship.

"At least, that's what it says in the book on being a stage director," he added.

"Working off a cheat sheet, huh!" cackled Tsuburaba. Cheating or not, Honenuki was determined to keep his cast and crew's eyes on the prize.

"Think about how hard we worked, leading up to

today. Personally, I don't want our show cut off unceremoniously before the end."

Ever since deciding to put on a theatrical production, class B had labored in the hours after school, on their days off, and during every free minute, all for this single performance. It meant a lot to them, and in that moment, Rin decided to speak on behalf of the group.

"All right. To the very end, then."

Class B was determined to make it work, and it was up to Honenuki to come up with a plan in far too little time.

"First, we need to get Tetsutetsu off the stage. That means distracting the audience for a second."

Monoma had gotten over his initial shock at Tetsutetsu's sickly state and was attempting to work it into the flow of the scene.

"What now? Do you cower at the sight of my blade, Count Paris?"

Shoda and Awase were still dumbstruck; all they

knew was that Tetsutetsu wouldn't be doing any more acting at the moment. Monoma glimpsed Honenuki off stage left, and just as he got the gist of the plan, lightning flashed, thunder roared, and the dragon took flight over the audience. While the crowd was busy screaming, one of Tsunotori's floating horns caught Tetsutetsu by his cloak and ferried him offstage. Within seconds, Kaibara was dashing out from stage left wearing that very same cloak.

"I'm filling in. Maybe until the very end, depending on how Tetsutetsu's feeling," whispered Kaibara stiffly, unable to hide his nerves over being chosen as an impromptu understudy. He was closest in height to Tetsutetsu, and he had memorized the entire script.

"Will you be okay?" asked a concerned Shoda.

"Oh, sure. Not like my heart's about to leap outta my throat," said Kaibara through gritted teeth.

"If it does, I'll pick it up and shove it right back in," said Monoma. "This is the climax of the entire show, so it's do or die. Be sure to make it good and dramatic, yes? It's time for class B to prove its mettle."

Between flashes of the stage lights, Monoma turned toward Honenuki and nodded. The director nodded

back and signaled for the crew to end the dragon's flight.

"Your pet dragon must realize its master's time is up, Count Paris! Now, I will have satisfaction!" said Monoma as he charged.

"L-listen to me, Romeo..." said Kaibara, managing to dodge.

"No, you've said enough!"

Kaibara's voice trembled a bit, but his draped hood and Monoma's seamless performance kept the audience from realizing there'd been a switch. Tsuburaba and Rin had escorted poor Tetsutetsu to the bathroom, but everyone else backstage was watching intently. Sensing Kaibara's nerves, Tsunotori and Shiozaki prayed for him.

"Fight, fight, Kaibara!"

"The Lord presents us with trials so that we may grow!"

Perhaps their prayers were heard, because Kaibara managed to hold it together in the meantime.

There wasn't much script left to get through. The dragon—enraged over its master's predicament—would attack Romeo, but Count Paris would take the hit instead, protecting his son. Then, the villain would go on to confess his sins and admit that he was in fact the king of another kingdom altogether before naming Romeo as his true heir. As king of two kingdoms, Romeo would vow to uphold peace, and he and Juliet would enjoy their fairy-tale ending.

On cue, the dragon charged at Romeo from behind the castle, and an already heavily wounded Paris cried "Watch out!" and dove between them.

"Count Paris, why would you...?"

"What father wouldn't shield his son from the evils of this world...?"

Kaibara was looking especially nervous about his upcoming monologue, so Monoma whispered, "I can feed you lines if you forget them." Kaibara nodded and started to speak.

"Long ago...I fell down a wicked path..."

Kaibara struggled to remember the lines and faltered here and there, but the audience mistook this for a masterful portrayal of a man on the verge of death. They learned of the unfortunate events that plagued this villain's life, his regrets, and his penitence, which elicited at least a bit of weepy sniffling from them. Seeing this, a proud look arose on Monoma's face, which Shoda and Awase quickly concealed by shifting their bodies. At one point, they noticed that Tetsutetsu had returned to the wings.

"Sorry, guys, but I'm good now!" he said to the rest of the class, with a much healthier look about him than a few minutes prior.

The others scolded him for worrying them but were plainly relieved.

"Yup, just had to get that bad fish outta my system, whatever it took. But how's Kaibara doing?"

"He's got the audience by their heartstrings!" said Tsuburaba.

"Whoa, nice!" said Tetsutetsu, glancing at Honenuki. "So I guess we'll let Kaibara finish it...?"

"No. If you're good to go, I'd rather it be your face they see when Paris dies."

Thinking that another use of the dragon as a distraction would seem shoehorned, Honenuki consulted the script.

"I've got it—instead of having our ring spirit descend from the catwalk, we'll have her come in from the back of the auditorium. That's when Tetsutetsu and Kaibara will swap places."

"In order to distract the audience again, I suppose?" said Shiozaki.

"We can do it!" added Tsunotori.

Satisfied with Honenuki's suggestion, Shiozaki and her would-be hippogriffs left for the rear of the auditorium. Honenuki tried to gesture to Kaibara about the swap, but the latter was too caught up in his monologue to notice. Fortunately, Monoma glimpsed the gesture and realized what it meant. When to make the swap, though? The monologue was about to end with Paris naming Romeo as his successor, so Monoma correctly guessed that the switch had to be timed with the next appearance of the ring spirit.

"Tetsutetsu is switching back in," he whispered hastily during a pause in Kaibara's lines.

At this, Kaibara swiveled his gaze toward stage left, spotted a cheery Tetsutetsu waving, and suddenly lost focus.

"Keep going, Kaibara. 'The one to inherit my kingdom will be...'" prompted Monoma, since Kaibara's instant relief seemed to have made him lose his place. He regained focus and—eager to finish his tenure as understudy—blurted out his final line.

"The one to inherit my kingdom will be...Juliet!"

"Huh?" said Monoma, a little louder than he meant

to. The audience also seemed confused by the twist this late in the show.

Kaibara knew he'd really stepped in it, and the color drained from his face. A number of the crew members offstage went pale too. The mistake was simple enough, but it had drastic implications for the plot.

"What now, Honenuki?" asked Tsuburaba.

"We still have to make the swap!"

It was now or never, so Honenuki gave his signal. On cue, Shiozaki emerged in the middle of the auditorium with Tsunotori and Shishida roaring and growling at her side. While the audience was distracted, Tetsutetsu dashed onto the stage, and Kaibara said "So sorry!" as he scampered off.

"Oh, Romeo…" said Shiozaki, as the spirit of the ring. "The power that resides within you must be used to achieve peace…"

All eyes were on Shiozaki and her divine presence, so the desperate actors onstage and the equally panicked crew backstage took the opportunity to figure out their next move.

Can we play it off as a joke? No, why would Paris crack a joke during his dramatic death scene… Ugh, what do we do?

Monoma didn't have long to think, because the crowd started murmuring in excitement. He realized they were staring at Kodai, who had descended from the castle's terrace and was now walking toward him.

"J-Juliet…?"

Kodai walked right past the stunned Monoma and grabbed the sword sheathed at Shoda's waist. Not a soul in the room could have anticipated what she would say when she turned and pointed the blade at Monoma.

"I challenge you to battle, for the right to the throne."

"Huhh?"

Seeing everyone so desperate, Kodai had been inspired to improvise.

"Why, Yui, why?" said Tokage, off stage left.

"A duel? What the heck?" said Tsuburaba. But the offstage crew couldn't run out to assist in any way; the cast was on its own—a fact that Tetsutetsu was painfully aware of.

"Th-the truth is, you two are half-siblings! I named Juliet my heir, but if she, um, seeks to win her throne in combat, so be it. The winner will inherit the crown and, like, rule in my stead!"

"Huhh?" gasped Monoma, indignant that their

carefully crafted plot had been totally upended. But Kodai shifted into a battle stance, showing no signs of backing down. Off to the side, Awase and Shoda realized they had to follow the story where Kodai had taken it.

"It's looking like Juliet means business! You've gotta stand up and fight, prince!" said Awase.

"The future of Gondur rests on your shoulders!" said Shoda.

"Very well. We will duel, *sister*."

"Indeed, *brother*…"

Forced into impromptu battle, Monoma picked up his sword and pointed it at Kodai.

Honenuki and the crew stood by in the wings, knowing they might have to leap into action at any moment to accommodate the improvisation.

The sword fight began, and it was anyone's guess how it would end.

What now? Should I win? Purposely lose…? More importantly, how do we bring this whole thing to a conclusion?

Monoma's train of thought was cut off, since Kodai's swordplay quickly had him cornered. He bumped up against the castle, rocking the dragon puppet off-balance and sending it toppling down toward Kodai.

"Nooo!"

He dove forward to shield her, and the direct hit knocked him out like one of Kendo's chops. All eyes were now on Kodai, wondering what she'd do next. Standing over the unconscious Monoma, she lifted her blade, turned, and brought it down across the dragon's neck. Fukidashi and Kamakiri were ready to provide some dramatic sound and light effects, in time with the action.

"My brother is avenged."

Though Kodai's face remained expressionless, her voice was tinged with rage and grief. Or so it seemed? Human emotions are important tools for coexisting with one another, so despite Kodai's blank face, monotone voice, and incomprehensible actions, human nature forced all those bearing witness to perceive the emotions that must be running through the character's head, effectively mobilizing their imaginations to fill in the gaps of the inexplicable. The audience saw what they wanted to see, and the rest of the class backstage was equally impressed.

"So Romeo sacrificed himself for her, and then she slayed the dragon that slayed him, shroom!"

"Even though she challenged him to a duel, she still loved her brother that much!"

"Still that blank Kodai face, but her voice, her eyes... They told the tale!"

"That girl's a regular thespian... A star is born!"

"I think we've just witnessed Yui's true awakening out there!"

The class found themselves relating to the characters they'd read about in comics about the world of theater that they'd been passing around ever since they'd decided to put on a play. Meanwhile, Kodai walked to center stage and surveyed the crowd.

"I vow to build a kingdom. Not my father's, not my brother's, but a new kingdom. One founded on the ideals of peace and hope!" she said.

At this valiant declaration, Tetsutetsu forgot that his character was meant to have died.

"Rock on, Juliet!" he cried.

"You have my sword!" said Awase, as Samwize.

"And my...sword, too! Literally!" said Shoda, as Froyo.

With that, Kodai raised the blade into the air.

"We will march into the future, together."

Seeing the birth of this new, gallant queen, the stunned audience began to clap, and the applause turned into a full-blown standing ovation accompanied by a flood of cheers.

The stage takes on a life of its own, and when a passionate—albeit slapdash—production meets an audience ready and willing to embrace the fantastic, the result is an explosion of inexplicable excitement and emotion.

Still struggling to overcome his sheer shock, Honenuki managed to press the button to bring the curtain down. The instant the fringe hit the floor, the members in the wings burst out onto the stage.

"That was nuts, Yui! But you pulled it off!"

"I had no clue how that was gonna end…"

"Is Monoma alive over there?"

As his classmates were congratulating each other and breathing sighs of relief, Monoma's eyes popped open and he immediately asked, "What happened?"

"Well, after you got knocked out…" started Honenuki.

The applause continued on the other side of the curtain, and upon hearing the whole story, Monoma said, "All's well that ends well, I suppose," with one of his usual coy grins.

"You're right about that," said Honenuki, sighing.

The others clapped their director on the back and congratulated him on a job well done, which earned them a strained smile.

"But we've got one last job," he said. "The curtain call."

Thankfully, the standing ovation hadn't ended, and the members of class B could still feel the waves of energy emanating from the thunderous applause. It had been an exhausting experience, but the response was inspiring enough to make them consider putting on another stage production someday.

Smiles were plastered on the faces of both cast and crew as the curtain rose one last time.

Part 4
Beauty Pageant

I wonder what act they're on?

Looking somewhat bored, Itsuka Kendo sat on a folding chair in the dressing room and glanced up at the wall clock; based on the time, class B's play would be about halfway done. A gentle breeze blew through the open window, ruffling the curtains. It was a beautiful October day, just warm enough to make one forget it was autumn.

As Kendo's pageant attendant, Reiko Yanagi sat nearby, holding on to bags with makeup and accessories. She noticed Kendo's gaze and spoke up.

"I hope the play's going well."

"Me too," said Kendo.

The two girls had watched the dress rehearsal the day before and found themselves moved by their classmates' efforts, so it was sure to be an amazing production, assuming nothing went wrong. A strained smile forced itself onto Kendo's face, half out of concern, and half in faith that all would be well. If she'd been feeling like her normal self, she might've responded to Yanagi with, "I bet they're killing it out there."

"Nervous?"

Yanagi could guess what was going through Kendo's head, so Kendo repaid her friend's concern with a broad smile before standing.

Yeah, this isn't like me at all.

"I'm great! We'd better get moving though. Lemme carry that?"

"Not a chance. It's almost time for the main event, Itsuka," said Yanagi, who also stood and made for the door before Kendo could insist on helping. Kendo felt awkward about her friend doting on her, and it showed on her face.

On her way to the dress rehearsal, she'd worn a dress several levels fancier than anything she was used to, covered up by only a thin events team windbreaker.

As Kendo walked down the hall, her new look earned stares and whispers from passing students making poor attempts to hide their obvious interest. The extra attention felt like needles pricking her all over.

How do other girls wear stuff that's so free and flowy…?

Neito Monoma and the rest of Kendo's classmates had heaped on the praise, and she'd known it wasn't empty flattery; they'd meant every word. Still, she felt like she'd never get used to wearing the dress.

I bet it comes as easy as breathing to someone like Yaoyorozu.

Kendo suddenly remembered her teammate during their internships, Momo Yaoyorozu. If anyone could slip into a fancy dress like she was born to do it, it would be little miss princess herself. Class A hadn't put forward a contestant for the beauty pageant, however.

This would be Kendo's first pageant, of course. She understood the excitement surrounding a bunch of young women competing to be the most beautiful, and as a woman herself, she could even respect that pursuit. But Kendo had never cared much about traditional notions of feminine beauty; her thing was more about being attractive and cool in ways that people typically associated with boys. Not that she wanted to *be* a boy. It was just about style, for her. The women competing in the beauty pageant, though, would naturally be judged on the basis of their feminine beauty.

Kendo had never dreamed of entering of her own accord. When class B's homeroom teacher, Vlad King, had told the class that the School Festival would feature a beauty pageant, the thought hadn't even crossed Kendo's mind. Rather, it had been Monoma's forceful recommendation that put things in motion.

"If anyone's entering the beauty pageant, it would have to be Kendo," he'd said.

The rest of the class had been convinced the moment Monoma uttered Kendo's name, practically ruling out any other candidate instantly.

"Hang on—that's way outta my wheelhouse," she'd said at the time.

But she understood that Monoma was out to make class B shine, and the rest of her classmates were just as excited. Kendo never would've entered for her own sake, but she didn't want to let the class down, so she'd reluctantly relented. Now that she was competing, of course she was aiming for the crown (or tiara, as it

were), but she still couldn't shake that nagging feeling that she didn't belong. She hadn't felt like herself since the day her name had been submitted for consideration.

Snap out of it!

As they reached the main greenroom behind the pageant stage, Kendo slapped her own cheeks with both hands to shake off the dark thoughts. At the sound of the slapping, Yanagi spun around in shock as if she'd seen a ghost.

"What on earth are you doing?"

"Just revving myself up."

"You're going to make your face all red!"

Yanagi put the bags down and placed her own hands on Kendo's cheeks. The pale girl's hands were as cold as the dead, and Kendo gave a slight shudder as they pressed against her warm face.

"What's going on, huh? Huh? Trying to chase the pain away?"

"Oh, hello, Nejire," said Yanagi.

Third-year Nejire Hado was staring at the two class B girls with a puzzled look.

"Nah, that's just how I rev myself up," said Kendo hurriedly, which earned a wide smile from Hado.

"Revving up, huh! Lemme try it! Hmph!" said Hado, clenching her fists and striking a power pose. Her own attendant, Yuyu Haya, smiled and raised an eyebrow.

"Careful, Nejire," she said. "Rev too hard and your Quirk might activate."

"Pfft, I know that."

"How's your throat doing?" asked Haya. "Want some jasmine tea?"

"Yup, yup, I could use some. Thanks."

As Hado gulped down the tea, Haya examined her earrings and headdress.

"I'm not too sure this is the right look for you..." she said, looking intense.

The sight of Hado—one of U.A.'s "Big Three"—acting surprisingly down to earth made Kendo and the other nervous pageant contestants smile and relax a little in spite of themselves. For all her charisma and skills, Hado came off as perfectly charming and relatable.

At that moment, another charismatic contestant entered the room.

"Oh ho ho ho ho ho ho ho ho! How do you do, ladies?"

It was Bibimi Kenranzaki. A third-year in U.A.'s

Support Course, she'd been the beauty pageant winner for two years running, was the personification of beauty itself, and pursued splendiferousness in every facet of her life. People joked that her long, gorgeous eyelashes could serve as earthquake seismographs, lightning rods, or even landing beacons for UFOs, and her reputation for fabulosity had made her something of a living legend at U.A. High.

Kendo and the others found themselves momentarily blinded by Kenranzaki's splendor, as if they had stared at the sun.

"Today, we compete. I hope we all fight with no regrets left on the table!" said Kenranzaki.

"S-sure!"

"Y-yeah!"

Everyone besides Hado was suddenly all nerves, half out of delight from being graced with Kenranzaki's gorgeous presence, and half out of despair over the sudden realization that they had no chance in hell of winning the pageant. If Hado was a charming angel with a soothing aura, Kenranzaki was a terrible goddess whose beauty filled the air with a nameless tension. These two were on opposite ends of that particular aesthetic spectrum.

Kenranzaki approached Hado. The others held their breath at this meeting of last year's pageant queen and its runner-up.

"May the best woman win, Nejire."

"Mm-hmm, I'm counting on it, cuz I'm the best, and I've got no intention of losing."

At Hado's undaunted throwing of the gauntlet, Kenranzaki's long lashes twitched. Everyone glanced around, half expecting an earthquake, a lightning bolt, or a UFO landing.

"Ah, I'm so very sorry to inform you that victory will be mine once again this year. And shouldn't you think about changing into your dress soon?" said Kenranzaki.

"Uh, I'm already wearing it?" said Hado.

"Apologies! I mistook that plain old thing for your everyday garb! Oh ho ho ho ho ho ho ho ho!"

"That's just mean! I think my dress is cute, okay?"

Ooh... I can see the sparks flying already!

Most of Kendo's friends were as lighthearted and easygoing as she was, so she wasn't used to witnessing catty showdowns like this.

Just like a scene outta some manga or a soap opera.

She was almost curious, watching what seemed

like a scripted scene play out, whereas the rest of the young women present froze up, unsure how best to dodge the flying sparks.

It's not like they're gonna start throwing punches, but maybe I should step in?

Kendo's big-sisterly instincts flared, but just before she could intervene, someone else made a move.

"Scuse me, Kenranzaki, but could I ask you to back off of Nejire?"

"Yuyu?" said a shocked Hado.

Haya had rushed in like a loyal hunting dog ready to defend its master from a looming bear, and her tone showed that she was ready to sink her teeth into the threatening foe if need be. Kenranzaki and Hado had known exactly what sort of electricity they were sending into the air a second ago, but Haya's icy stare brought a new chill over the room. Not that it was enough to fluster Kenranzaki's beautiful composure.

"My dear Yuyu, as Nejire's attendant, shouldn't you be the one reining her in? Instead of…getting so bent out of shape yourself?"

The comeback left Haya at a loss for words, but she was saved by someone from the pageant planning committee, who entered the room and began explaining the dress rehearsal procedure. During the explanation, the girls heard the cawing of a crow coming from the extravagant outdoor stage. Not exactly a good omen.

In the meantime, Kendo stole a glance at Haya. Standing beside a flustered Nejire, Haya wore a scowl with eyes cast down.

I wonder what's up with Yuyu…?

They'd only met briefly at the pageant orientation, but Kendo had noted Haya's remarkable self-possession—befitting a third-year—which was somewhat at odds with her short, bleach-blond hair, multiple piercings, and generally eye-catching appearance. Being paired up with the free-spirited Hado only served to amplify Haya's levelheaded nature. When Kendo had introduced herself, Haya had smiled and offered to answer any questions Kendo might've had about the pageant, which had made her barefaced hostility just a moment ago all the more shocking.

Is this what became of women thrown into battle against one another? Kendo found herself thinking more than ever that if that was the case, then she really didn't belong there.

The dress rehearsal ended without incident, and the contestants returned to their individual greenrooms. Kendo let out a long, pent-up sigh.

"Pretty intense out there," said Yanagi, not sounding particularly amused—more like she was making a simple observation.

"Yeah. Caught me off guard... But I should've known."

"Known what?"

"Erm, never mind. Forget it."

Yanagi's look seemed to ask, "Are you sure it's nothing?" But Kendo smiled, shook her head, and changed the subject.

"How'd I do?" she asked, referring to the little preview of her pageant performance. Kendo herself didn't know if she wanted to talk about the competitive aspects or chat about how she felt so out of place, and she feared that in this unsure state, anything she said would come off as pointless complaining.

"It looked really clean, I thought. But is the hem of that dress too tight?" asked Yanagi.

"It's fine. This kata doesn't feature too many wide stances," said Kendo.

For the talent show part of the competition, she'd chosen to perform a martial arts routine. Kendo had racked her brain trying to think of a way to showcase her feminine sensibilities, but when she'd come up short, she had settled on doing something she knew she was good at. After all, the other contestants would be highlighting their own special skills through dance, song, or what have you. Each had done a small portion of her act during the rehearsal (leaving the full performances for the pageant itself), though an apparently unconcerned Kenranzaki had skipped the rehearsal altogether, saying only, "I look forward to the main event!"

"Are you hungry? Want anything for lunch?" asked Yanagi.

"Not really. I'll wait 'til it's all over. But you should eat, Reiko."

"I'm not that hungry either, honestly."

As they sat around chatting while waiting for the show to begin, Kendo and Yanagi heard someone cry "What the hell is this?" from the next greenroom over. They locked eyes and raced to the source.

"Um, what's the matter?" asked Kendo, peeking into the room. Hado looked upset, and beside her, Haya had a high heel in one hand and a large nail in the other. Her face was practically quivering with rage.

"This nail was in one of Nejire's shoes…" said Haya.

"Whoa!" said Kendo.

"This is sabotage, I know it!" said Haya, unable to hide her anger.

"Hmm," said Hado. "How can we know for sure, though? Maybe it just fell in there."

"Fell? From where? Nuh-uh. That doesn't just happen," spat Haya. Kendo had to agree it was unlikely, but she wasn't fully ready to accept the sabotage theory. The nail was huge. Too big for intentional sabotage, since the would-be victim would be sure to notice it before slipping the shoe on. A thumbtack would've worked, maybe? But a nail was just begging to be discovered. Still, Haya had lost all composure and was convinced that someone was out to hurt Hado.

"Probably that Kenranzaki…" said Haya with a start. Hado's face grew dark.

"Cut that out. We have no proof," she said.

"Sorry. But c'mon… The former winner has the most to gain by making sure you're out of the running…"

"I said, cut it out," repeated Hado sternly, leaving Haya unable to respond. Just as Kendo was feeling awkward about witnessing the minor spat, a nearby voice cried, "Well, search harder, please!" All four girls looked at each other and stepped out to see what was up.

"What's wrong in here?" asked Kendo.

"Oh. You ladies," said Kenranzaki. "Well...I cannot find the necklace I'm meant to wear for the main event. It was on that table until the dress rehearsal! I will swear to that!"

She pointed to a jewelry box on the table near the windowsill. Meanwhile, her attendants were scurrying about, searching every nook and cranny of the room. The shadow of a bird raced across the curtains fluttering in the wind.

"Was the door unlocked? And the window open?" asked Kendo.

"Unlocked, yes, but only while I stepped out for a brief moment," admitted Kenranzaki.

It seemed like a careless thing to do, but it wasn't as if Kendo or Hado had locked their own greenrooms. Since this was all happening within the safety of the school grounds, most of the contestants weren't being particularly vigilant.

What if it was *a thief, though?*

As the thought crossed Kendo's mind, Yanagi muttered to herself.

"Looks like it's true…"

"What's true?" asked Kendo, who'd overheard.

"That these pageants are rife with sabotage," said Yanagi. Her main hobby was surfing the internet, and Yanagi had done some reading about beauty pageants in her free time. Apparently, mudslinging and dirty deeds were common occurrences behind the scenes.

"Though I guess we don't know for sure yet," added Yanagi.

"Yeah, but this is no laughing matter…" said Kendo with a bit of an edge to her voice. Whether it was all part of some devious plan or not, a nail had found its way into a shoe and jewelry had gone missing. It wasn't a huge stretch to connect the two incidents.

Sabotage, though…? How would we even deal with that…?

The trashy tabloids would start licking their chops upon hearing of backstage scandal and intrigue at U.A.'s beauty pageant. But were these young women really like that? As boys would tell it, girls were prone to fighting their battles in sneaky, underhanded ways, and not in the light of day. Kendo didn't think she was that sort of woman, but how could she be sure?

Woman.

To Kendo, the very word often felt like a burden. She preferred to be defined on her own terms. Plenty of men felt the same way, no doubt, while some people out there felt like they didn't fit snugly into either discrete category. It was like somebody, at some point, had decided to stuff everyone into these cramped, preconceived pigeonholes, where women had to be one way, and men another. The whole notion was obnoxious, in Kendo's opinion.

Hmm? Men... Obnoxious... Obnoxious men...

Switching tracks on her train of thought, Kendo saw a certain face rise in her mind's eye. An obnoxious guy who took gleeful jabs at class A whenever the chance arose. Monoma.

"Listen, Kendo! You have to win this!" he'd said, shortly after she'd agreed to compete in the pageant. "Your victory will prove class B's worth to the entire school! To that end, you have my full support! Whatever it takes!"

Recalling Monoma's words, Kendo went pale. She had 99 percent faith that he wouldn't stoop that low, but she couldn't discount the possibility outright.

What if sabotaging the other girls is Monoma's idea of "supporting" me?

If Monoma's deranged love for class B had led him to such vile actions, it was Kendo's job to find him and put a stop to it all with a swift chop to the neck. At that moment, though, the girls in the greenroom heard heavy footsteps just outside.

"Has anyone seen my baby's remote control?" screamed Mei Hatsume, wearing a grimy tank top and running at a breakneck pace. "Hey, Kenranzaki! Have you seen it?" she said.

"What on earth are you talking about, Mei? And despite my repeated admonishing, have you still not bathed?" said Kenranzaki.

"I was up all night tinkering!" said Hatsume.

Seeing the mad inventor run right up to Kenranzaki, Kendo recalled that they were both members of the Support Course.

"Very well. What's this about a remote control?" asked Kenranzaki with a resigned look, knowing that trying to convince Hatsume to focus on anything besides her inventions would be a losing battle.

"The remote for my super-duper cute baby #202 that I'm exhibiting at the festival!"

If U.A.'s Sports Festival was where the Hero Course got to shine, then the School Festival was meant as a platform for General Studies, the Business Course, and the Support Course to strut their stuff. The Support Course, in particular, garnered plenty of attention for their time-honored tech exhibition, which members of all grades helped put together. The guest list this year included only a small number of outside parties, but those handpicked industry bigwigs would still be expecting a lot from the exhibition, even if it was on a smaller scale than usual. If a Support Course student's inventions could catch the eyes of these visitors, that student could very well expect multiple job offers upon graduation, so Hatsume was understandably upset over her predicament. Without that remote, she couldn't show off her prized invention.

"Well, it's not here. We were just scouring the room for my necklace, so I'm sure we would have come across your remote," said Kenranzaki.

"Gah!" yelped Hatsume.

"What, you didn't think to create a spare one?"

"A spare? I was too busy working R&D to think about spares!"

"I assume you searched the studio already?"

"Of course! And the classroom and the dorms and the cafeteria and the bathrooms! Everywhere I've been! This was my last hope!"

"Why were you *here*?"

"You told me I oughta add some more sparkle to my babies, so I dropped by to watch you in action and learn a thing or two! But you weren't here! Argh, what do I do, Kenranzaki? The exhibition's about to start! Don't tell me I gotta operate my baby by hand? Or maybe it actually would be more effective if I just climbed inside and did it all manually?"

With far too little sleep powering her, Hatsume's bloodshot eyes bulged from their sockets. Rattling on and on at top speed, she resembled a robot in the process of short-circuiting. Observing this, Kenranzaki walked up to Hatsume and made use of her impressive eyelashes. As Kenranzaki's luscious lashes descended from above, they gently forced closed Hatsume's eyes (she hadn't blinked since showing up) as well as her mouth, which had been spraying flecks of saliva all about.

"Mmrgh?" mumbled Hatsume.

"We of the Support Course must at all times strive for beauty!" barked Kenranzaki.

Her lashes withdrew from Hatsume's own eyelids, allowing the younger girl to blink again.

"Now calm yourself, and I will help you search," continued Kenranzaki, decisively. It was Kendo's turn to look wide eyed.

"Are you sure? What about the pageant?" she asked.

"We still have time," declared Kenranzaki.

Hado, who'd been watching the back-and-forth from the sidelines in silence, raised her hand.

"Yup, yup, I'll help too," she said.

"Seriously, Nejire?" said Haya. Hado grinned.

"The more people looking, the better our odds of finding it," she said, as if that were the only reasonable response. Kendo gasped.

"Um, me too," she said hastily.

"My, my..." said Kenranzaki. "All of you, then?"

"Sure, but let's be quick about it," said Kendo.

"Thank you so much, girls!" said Hatsume, who'd

finally recovered a modicum of composure. Kenranzaki asked if there was anywhere else she'd been that morning, which sparked Hatsume's memory.

"I forgot about the woods! I ran through there on my way back!"

Once one of Kenranzaki's attendants had explained the situation to a pageant committee member, the girls were off to the races. As Kendo ran, she apologized to Yanagi for implicitly volunteering her services too.

"Why should I stay behind just because I'm an attendant? Plus, I figured you would offer to help, Itsuka," said Yanagi.

"Thanks for understanding," said Kendo, before glancing back at Haya, who was running a few paces behind. Haya had looked ready to protest when Hado had volunteered but had remained silent in the end. Fully in search mode, Hado was asking Hatsume what the remote looked like.

Are they fighting...? Nah, that couldn't be it.

Haya was looking grumpier than ever, with a fully furrowed brow.

"Huh? Where are you off to, Hado?" came a voice. It was Tamaki Amajiki, who, as another of Hado's pageant helpers, was on his way to the greenrooms. He agreed to help after a quick explanation, opting to use his Manifest Quirk to sprout wings (courtesy of quail eggs he'd eaten from a stall earlier) and search from the air.

"Thanks again for helping out, everyone," said Hatsume. "Now let's find my super-duper cute baby's remote control!"

Upon reaching the woods, the group split up to search along Hatsume's approximate route.

"Dratted tree branch… Hmph," said Kenranzaki. Her eyelashes had gotten caught on a branch, but she quickly freed herself with lash power alone and kept searching. Since she maintained proper posture while minding her flowing dress, Kenranzaki's search effort almost resembled an elaborate contemporary dance.

Seeing this, Kendo was reminded of Kenranzaki's resolute offer to help. This was a day when the older girl no doubt wanted to focus entirely on herself, but she had still set aside everything to aid a first-year without a second thought. Kendo thought that was cooler than cool. The way Hado had done it, too. It took a certain strength of character to step up and help a virtual stranger when they were in a pinch.

"Come to me, remote!" cried Hatsume, crawling around on all fours nearby.

"Don't worry, we'll find it," said Kendo.

"Thanks, I sure hope so! Because this baby of mine just *has to* make a good showing today! This little one is really amazing—useful in just about any situation, and simple enough that anyone can handle it, no matter their Quirk!"

Hatsume's stomach gave an unearthly growl.

"Did you skip breakfast, by chance?" asked Kendo.

"Erm, come to think of it, I haven't had a thing since yesterday. Also forgot to get any shut-eye!"

"Huh? How are you still standing?"

"Relax, I'll eat and sleep for ages once this is all over, to make up for the past forty-eight hours."

So Hatsume had been tinkering nonstop for two days straight? Kendo was beyond impressed by that sort of abnormal focus.

"Is everyone in the Support Course as dedicated as you?"

"Plenty of us can get kinda obsessive, yeah, but Kenranzaki is different," said Hatsume. "She eats and sleeps according to a real strict schedule and only gets in focus mode during set times. That's the most beautiful way to live, she says. But judging from her bold, cutting-edge, dazzling designs, I would've guessed she regularly skips whole weeks' worth of sleep, if I didn't know better! Her work's already earned her a whole pack of crazed fans, y'know!"

The Hatsume talk train was roaring out of the station, and she was now up in Kendo's face.

"But even while working, Kenranzaki is always looking out for us in all sorts of ways! Sure, her 'You ought to bathe once in a while, Hatsume' routine gets old real quick, but otherwise, she's a role model I know I can rely on!"

"Hatsume, focus!" came Kenranzaki's chiding voice. Speak of the devil.

Hatsume gasped, came to her senses, and resumed her frenzied search.

Not the type who can multitask, I take it.

Kendo got back to searching too, wanting to help more than hinder. She advanced slowly—checking between every tree and bush as she went—but soon bumped into something soft that went, "Huh?"

"Oops, sorry, Yuyu…"

"Oh. Kendo… Don't sweat it," said Haya, who hadn't shaken that scowl from a moment ago. Kendo wasn't sure if it'd be appropriate to ask, so she kept searching in silence.

"Hey. Sorry about earlier, if I made things weird," said Haya, who also didn't seem so sure about speaking up.

"What? Oh, that's cool! Don't worry!"

"No, I know how high strung I can get. Kenranzaki was right—I *am* bent out of shape…" said Haya with a self-deprecating chuckle. Kendo now understood that the girl's scowl had been directed at herself.

"I'm willing to listen while we search, if you wanna talk," said Kendo.

"Sure, if you don't mind," said Haya with a bitter smile. "I was the one who suggested Nejire compete in the pageant, originally. I mean, have you seen her? Total cutie. I was sure she'd bring home the crown, but then she lost to Kenranzaki two years in a row. Not that she did anything wrong. If those judges can't see how cute she is, their eyes must be malfunctioning, cuz nobody in our whole damn galaxy can hold a candle to Nejire!"

Haya seemed to be thinking back on those bitter

losses, because she started snorting in indignation. She went on, stressing how undeniably cute it was when Hado did this, that, or just about anything.

It's like she's bragging about her amazing sweetheart?

It warmed Kendo's heart to see this third-year's eyes sparkle in admiration, but suddenly Haya's face grew dark.

"So this whole time, I've been feeling like I went and got her hurt for nothing... Pageant or no pageant, Nejire's still just as cute, right? But this year, she said she *wanted* to compete and she wanted to win. I want that for her so bad I'd do just about anything, but when I get so worked up and worry her like that... Ugh, I'm the worst. I'm usually more put together, you know? As we've gotten closer and closer to the big day, I've felt my fuse getting shorter and shorter, like I'm not even myself..."

Kendo wished she could cheer up Haya, but she couldn't find the words. In all honestly, she didn't feel like herself either.

"Yuyu."

"Nejire...?"

Hado peeked out from behind a nearby tree, and the

strange look on her face told the tale; she'd overheard everything.

"Nejire, I…"

"Listen, Yuyu…"

The two girls started to talk simultaneously, but a cry from Amajiki interrupted them.

"Hey, I found the culprit!"

The culprit?

Everyone glanced at each other before running in the direction of Amajiki's voice.

"Where?" shouted Hatsume and Kenranzaki in unison, only to spot Amajiki up in the air, flying away from a cawing crow that was after him.

"Huh?"

"A crow?"

"What do you mean?" asked the confused girls.

Amajiki pointed to the branch of a nearby tree, where they spotted a necklace and Hatsume's shiny remote control.

"There it is! My baby's remote!"

"And that would be my jewelry!"

"I remember hearing something about how crows are attracted to shiny objects," said Amajiki, still fighting off the bird.

"You're saying our thief is a crow?" said Kendo, shocked to learn the identity of the unlikely culprit. The girls were thrilled, though. Once Amajiki grabbed the items, it would be case closed.

"Cawww!"

It wasn't that simple, however. The crow continued to harangue Amajiki, as it could sense that he was out to steal back its hard-earned stash.

"Hey. Cut that out. That stuff's not yours to begin with... Yikes, get away from me!"

Amajiki was equipped with any number of ways to battle villains, but he'd never fought a bird before, let alone one of the smartest birds around. This crow knew it couldn't beat the human attempting to steal its treasures, so while Amajiki was flailing in midair, it swooped down, deftly grabbed Kenranzaki's necklace and Hatsume's remote in its beak, and flew off in the opposite direction. The girls gave chase, tracking the bird from the ground.

"Sorry... Crows are actually pretty scary up close..." apologized Amajiki.

"Not a problem," said Hado, who activated her own "Surge" Quirk and rose into the air on spiraling waves

of energy. She sped ahead, cut the crow off, grabbed the necklace and remote right out of its mouth, and left it in her dust.

"Thanks a ton, whoever you are!" said Hatsume.

"Uh-huh, I'm Nejire Hado."

"Look out, Hado!" cried Amajiki, alerting her just in time to see the enraged crow coming at her.

"Eek!"

She dodged the bird's attack by a hair, but it had plenty more where that came from. The crow kept up its assault, all the while cawing at an earsplitting volume.

"Oh no, Nejire..." said a worried Yuyu.

Desperate to help, Kendo used her "Big Fist" Quirk to enlarge her hands, but since the bird was out of reach up above, all she could do was flap her hands to create small air blasts. One of these knocked the offender for a loop, but before everyone knew it, a murder of several dozen crows had emerged from nowhere, chasing not only the airborne Amajiki and Hado, but also the gang on the ground. It seemed the original offender had caw-called for its birds of a feather.

"Whoa! Back off, birds!" cried Kendo, covering her friends with one massive hand while attempting to shoo away the crows with the other. She could've smacked them out of the air with ease, but since these weren't actually villains, Kendo was trying to avoid harming the animals. Hado and Amajiki were of the same mind, which left them unsure how to cope. Suddenly, Kenranzaki ran by and shouted, "This will just take a moment!" A good portion of the murder chased after her, drawn in by her glimmering, ornate hairpin, which she plucked from her head and tossed while crying, "You can have it!"

Meanwhile, Hado was under siege, desperately defending the remote and the necklace. Unable to restrain herself, Haya ran over and said, "Nejire, throw them to me!"

"Or me!" screamed Hatsume, who'd also been tracking Hado. "Once I've got 'em, I'll show these birds how fast I can run!"

Watching this scene play out, Kendo paused to think. The tech exhibition was about to begin, so the priority was putting the remote in Hatsume's hands and getting her to the show.

"Give Hatsume the remote, and I'll catch as many crows as I can," shouted Kendo toward Hado and Amajiki.

"Me and Amajiki can shoo away the rest, sure. You good with that, Amajiki?" said Hado.

"Um, yeah. I like that plan better than just being pecked at forever," said Amajiki with a weak nod. Hado looked for an opening and tossed the remote toward Hatsume.

"Ahh, my precious baby's remote!" cried Hatsume, who caught the device and made a break for it. The bulk of the murder noticed the transfer and gave chase, but Kendo was ready; she scooped a number of crows out of the air and slammed her enormous cupped hand to the ground, forming a small, sealed dome. While Hado and Amajiki were attempting to drive off the rest of the birds, Hatsume stumbled and fell in a grand fashion.

"Ack!"

Kendo's body moved on instinct to help Hatsume, and before she could stop herself, the seal of her hand dome broke ever so slightly, allowing the trapped crows to escape and resume their assault on the others.

Ugh, what'm I even doing?

But Kendo didn't have long to blame herself, because the ground started rumbling.

"What on earth?" said Yanagi with wide eyes.

A massive tank shaped like Kenranzaki's face was approaching from the nearby path, sending the crows into a confused panic.

"Oh ho ho ho ho ho ho ho ho! How do you like this, you awful avians?"

"Kenranzaki?"

Riding atop the metallic face was Kenranzaki herself.

"Wuzzat? Wow, so cool!" said Hado, prompting a smug Kenranzaki to explain.

"My creation for the talent portion of the pageant, of course. It's my Beautiful Perfect Gorgeous Armored Vehicle! I had hoped to unveil it for the first time during the show, but alas—I would do anything for a fellow member of the Support Course!"

Every surface of Kenranzaki's tank glittered and glistened, and in the sunlight, one might have mistaken the shining mass for some sort of deity incarnate.

What had Kenranzaki created this thing to do, exactly? Questions swirled in the minds of everyone present, except for Hatsume, who shouted like a child might at the appearance of a hero.

"Go get 'em, Kenranzaki!"

The maddened crows were driven into a further frenzy by the largest shiny object yet, which they now made a beeline for.

"Watch out!" cried Kendo, dashing over to help, but Kenranzaki calmly pushed a button on her control panel.

"Dine on this! Goddess Zephyr!" screamed Kenranzaki, as if naming an ultimate move. The robot's eyelashes began to flap up and down, instantly creating a series of complex air currents that caught the murder in their grasp and flung the birds high into the air, as if by a passing tornado. Everyone's jaws dropped, and Kenranzaki pressed another button.

"Now, come quietly! Confectionary Sigh!"

This time, the robot launched a lacy net of glittery white thread from its mouth that enveloped the crows and sent them hurtling to the ground. But just before impact, a small parachute popped open, making for a gentle landing. An image of Kenranzaki's face decorated the parachute too, of course.

Kendo was dumbfounded by this capture operation that had come in like a sudden squall and subdued the crows without harming a feather on their heads.

"These corvidae cretins certainly gave us a run for our money," said Kenranzaki, finally putting her stolen necklace back on.

"There's one more thing, though…" said Haya. She reached into her pocket and took out the nail they'd found in the high heel earlier.

"Where'd this come from, huh?"

"Why, we use those nails in the Support Course," said Kenranzaki.

"Oh yeah?"

"But the only person using ones of that size at the moment is…Mei."

Prompted by Kenranzaki, Hatsume took a look at the nail.

"Huh? Ohh, yeah. When I dropped by your greenroom this morning, I stuck that nail in a shoe—where I knew you'd find it—to let you know I'd been there."

"Why the shoe?" said Haya.

"Well, it might've rolled right off the table, right? But she'd be sure to notice it while putting on her heels."

"Yes, but why a nail?"

"Kenranzaki's in the Support Course too, so she knows the nails I use better than anyone! But I guess

I picked the wrong greenroom? Oops, sorry! Anyway, I'm short on time, so we'll have to pick this up again later! Thanks so much for the help, everyone!"

Hatsume's feet were already moving as she said her thanks, and she raced off to the exhibition with remote in hand. She was out of sight by the time Kenranzaki shouted "Take a bath, you!" one final time.

"I must also thank you for assisting my first-year," said Kenranzaki to the rest of the group.

Seeing her polite bow, Kendo blurted, "No prob! Really."

"Yeah, more importantly..." said Hado, her eyes swiveling up to the Kenranzaki face tank. "What the heck *is* this thing, Kenranzaki? It's nuts!" She could hardly contain her childlike excitement.

"Oh ho ho ho ho ho ho ho ho! So you're a fan of my armored vehicle? If you truly appreciate my work, say the word, and I will create a support item or two just for you."

"Nah, your stuff's not my style."

"Hmph! You have no eye for beauty, in that case!" said Kenranzaki, suddenly in a huff over this differing of opinions.

"Nejire's a little more minimalist. More cutesy than gaudy," said Haya, trying to explain, but still seemingly holding back a bit, like she'd been doing all day. Hado walked over, smiled, and made a declaration in her usual innocent way.

"And you're you, Yuyu."

"Huh?"

"That's what I wanted to say before. You were all like, 'I'm not myself,' but even when you're not acting like yourself, that's still part of you, Yuyu. Even when you get all anxious or when you wish you were another way—that's the whole package, and that package is my good friend."

Kendo's eyes grew wide.

All just parts of the package, huh?

"But what if I hate some parts of myself?" asked Haya, looking enraged and miserable all at once. Hado mimed slapping her own cheeks and glanced at Kendo as she responded.

"At those times…rev yourself up!"

Kendo recalled her own cheek-slapping routine from earlier.

"How would that help?"

"Well, cuz it's all about taking that stuff you don't like and seeing it in a better light! Like, I'm going on and on about wanting to win this pageant cuz I know how happy that'd make you, Yuyu. And cuz I can't just sit back and accept being a runner-up!"

"I guess you *are* a sore loser, Nejire."

"Yup, so I'm gonna rev myself up, and I'm gonna win this thing!" declared Nejire, puffing out her chest.

"Careful, Nejire—your Quirk's gonna squirt out," said Haya with a smile, and the smile gave way to tears rising in the corners of her eyes. After this pep talk from her dear friend, she had no choice but to keep doing her best.

"Um, Kenranzaki, I'm...sorry, about before..."

"Think nothing of it, oh ho ho ho ho ho ho ho ho!" said Kenranzaki, laughing off Haya's timid apology.

Thinking hard on Hado's words and seeing these smiling faces around her, Kendo felt a sudden lightness in her own chest. She might not feel like herself sometimes, but there was no denying those other facets. Even when she didn't feel feminine enough or when trying to be someone she wasn't put her in a funk. That was still all her.

I'm always gonna be me, since there's nobody else I can be. And I'm good with that. I'm good with who I am.

At that moment, a pageant committee member ran over to the group in a panic.

"You're all contestants, right? We've been searching for you high and low! The show's about to begin!"

Kenranzaki turned to Hado and Kendo.

"Let us give them a noble, proper, and—above all else—beautiful show to remember!"

"As gorgeous and magnificent as the kanji in your name?" asked Hado with a grin. Kenranzaki smiled back, and the group hurried off to the stage. Watching the two older girls run, Kendo felt a relaxed smile emerge on her own face.

"What's up?" asked Yanagi, noticing Kendo's expression.

"I'm gonna tackle this *as me*. The best way I know how."

Kendo realized that Kenranzaki and Hado weren't competing on the basis of some preconceived notion of feminine beauty; what they were pitting against each other was what made each of them beautiful. If anything, those two were shining examples of being true to oneself.

"Hmm? Itsuka, your dress..." said Yanagi in a tone tinged with mild horror.

"Huh? Oh. It's ripped."

Indeed, the hem of her dress had a tear in it, probably from getting caught on a branch while she was crawling around in the woods.

"I'll have to mend it really quickly," said Yanagi, half in a panic, but Kendo thought for a moment and turned down the offer.

"That's okay. I'm probably gonna rip it even worse later."

"You sure?"

"Yeah. And actually—remember that extra lumber they had, after building the set for the play? You think that's still lying around somewhere?"

With a new plan to showcase what made her, her, Kendo smiled again. Gleaming in the sun, hers was the face of someone aiming for the top.

Part 5
Festival For All

"First, that one lady flew up in the air like FWOOOSH, all pretty-like! And then that one lady had a giant face that was the same as her face! And the other one broke all that wood with her hand like KRAK KRAK KRAK! And then, and then..."

An excited Eri talked a mile a minute while Izuku Midoriya and Mirio Togata nodded encouragingly.

Midoriya had had quite a day already. He'd foiled a U.A. infiltration plan by Gentle Criminal—a self-styled "gentleman scoundrel" who was prone to uploading videos of his capers on the internet with the help of his partner in crime, La Brava. After stopping the villain, the boy had still made it back in time to join class A's live performance—a showstopper that had succeeded in putting a smile back on Eri's face.

Now that the beauty pageant was over, everyone was splitting up to enjoy the sights and sounds of the festival. Midoriya and Togata had promised to spend the day with Eri, and joining them were Ochaco Uraraka, Tsuyu Asui, and chaperone Shota Aizawa—all of whom had joined the coalition to rescue Eri in the first place. Everyone present knew how much pain Eri had endured before they'd plucked her from her circumstances, so a simple smile from the small girl was enough to warm their hearts. And there was plenty more fun in store.

"Where would you like to go next, Eri?" asked Izuku, spreading out the festival pamphlet. Dozens of themed stalls and attractions dotted the user-friendly map, prompting Eri to squint and furrow her brow.

"Too many choices…"

"No prob!" said Togata. "We'll just starting walking, and if something catches your eye, give a shout!"

"Uh-huh," said the girl with a nod.

"Here, Eri," said Midoriya, extending his hand. "Grab my hand so you don't get lost out here." It was a legitimate concern, given the hustle and bustle in the

lane populated by food stalls, but Eri only stared at Midoriya's scarred hand.

"Ack, sorry! My hand's a little scary, huh?" he said, convinced that the scars had frightened the girl. But before he could pull it back, Eri reached out, grabbed his hand with both of hers, and shook her head back and forth.

"Not scary… It's a really nice hand that helped me," she muttered, catching Midoriya off guard.

"Oh, glad to hear it," he said with a relieved smile that drew another smile from Eri.

"And, what? *My* hand's just gotta be all lonely over here on its own?" said Togata.

"No way!" yelped Eri, grabbing Togata's hand and beaming at him.

The two boys locked eyes, said "Heave ho!" and lifted Eri into the air as they started walking.

"Wheee!" cried Eri as she bounced along, thrilled to be hand in hand with her two favorite heroes in the whole wide world.

"Aww, they look like a family!" remarked Uraraka, watching the trio from behind.

"Like two older brothers? And their much younger sister? Ribbit," said Asui.

Walking alongside the two girls, Aizawa's expression relaxed ever so slightly.

It had been an uphill battle to hold the School Festival at all this year. If U.A. were attacked again during the big event, society would lose even more faith in heroes—faith that was already on shaky ground in light of All Might's official retirement. And if people perceived that heroes lacked the stopping power they'd once held, villains would run rampant and society would devolve into chaos. Sensing this danger, law enforcement officials had strongly recommended that U.A. skip its festival this year, but Principal Nezu had argued that now, more than ever, the students had to believe in a bright future.

Even with that hurdle out of the way, it hadn't been a given that Eri could attend, but Aizawa had secured permission for this special guest once the school had been officially assigned as her guardian for the time being. It was the adults' job to protect the kids and their future, and Eri's smile reaffirmed that thought in Aizawa's mind. For both its newest pint-sized resident and the student body at large, U.A. had to be a bastion of safety and hope.

"Ooh, crepes!"

"What's *crehpz*?"

Uraraka's cry of joy upon spotting a crepe stall made a confused Eri whip around.

"You're in for a treat, Eri! A crepe is like a really, really thin pancake, loaded up with fresh cream and topped with fruit! It's the fanciest, heavenliest dessert around!"

"Crehpz sound yummy!" said Eri, practically with stars in her eyes.

"Why don't we get some, then?" suggested Asui, approaching the stall.

The menu of plastic sample items displayed standard toppings like banana, peach, tangerine, and chocolate, but Eri stared and timidly asked, "Is there...one with apples...?" Sadly, there wasn't.

"Don't worry!" said Togata, trying to cheer up the crestfallen girl. "We're still gonna find you a candy apple later!"

Midoriya twitched.

"Okay!" said Eri, the reminder of the candy apple bringing another smile to her face. As she deliberated over crepe choices, Togata made a declaration.

"Let me guess which one you'll choose, Eri! This time...it's gotta be peach! Peach, for sure!"

"No. Tangerine."

"That was my next guess! Hang on—you got something against peaches or what?"

After much deliberation of her own, Uraraka chose chocolate, and Asui went for banana.

"So sweet and yummy…" said Eri as she nibbled, with eyes closed in pure joy. Everyone felt their hearts grow a few sizes again.

Still eating their crepes, the gang entered the school. A live stand-up event caught Togata's eye, and amid all the hubbub, Midoriya saw something that got his attention too.

"A hero quiz competition… And the prize is a board signed by all the pro hero teachers at U.A.?"

The event was put together by some other class, and surely enough, the grand prize was a board covered in hero autographs, starting with All Might himself. Even Aizawa had signed, as Eraser Head. Seeing the stunned Midoriya's jaw drop, Aizawa said, "It's just some autographs."

"'Just autographs'? You take that back, Sensei!" said Midoriya with an indignant snort, ever the hero fanboy. "This is a rare, one-of-a-kind collectible,

featuring autographs from both All Might and Erasure Hero: Eraser Head, who rarely shows his face! And look—Present Mic, Vlad King, Midnight, Thirteen, Cementoss, Ectoplasm, Snipe, Power Loader, and Recovery Girl! Why, I've never even seen an autograph collection like this in *Heroes Monthly*!"

"Uh-huh. Sure," said Aizawa, deftly deflecting Midoriya's enthusiasm.

But I show my face to him every day of the week.

To Midoriya, there was apparently some sort of subtle, nuanced difference between Aizawa Sensei the homeroom teacher and Eraser Head the hero, whether the man himself understood it or not.

"Hey, they're still accepting entrants for the quiz!" said Uraraka.

"Erm, but…" stammered Midoriya.

"Get in there, man! We'll have a blast watching you, won't we, Eri?" said Togata.

"Uh-huh," said Eri with a nod. She was a little lost, but she'd understood that Midoriya might take home a cool prize if he won the contest.

"You can do it, Deku!" she added shyly.

"Well, that settles it! I'll give it my best shot, Eri!" said Midoriya.

With Eri's blessing, he marched up to the registry desk, got in line with the other entrants, and took a seat at a desk with a quick-draw buzzer button on it.

"Deku! Go for the gold!" shouted Uraraka.

"You've got this, Midoriya. Ribbit!" said Asui.

The student serving as quizmaster emerged to cheers from the audience. Once the excitement died down, the quiz began.

"Question one!" said the quizmaster. "Kamui Woods is a rising young star of the hero world. During his debut, what did he—"

Midoriya's button lit up with a "ding-ding."

"He captured a gang of bank robbers with his Preemptive Binding Lacquered Chain Prison!"

"Midoriya of class 1-A, youuu are correct! Moving on, question two! Flame Hero: Endeavor's favorite food is—"

Ding-ding.

"*Kuzumochi*!"

"Correct again!"

The other contestants hadn't stood a chance against Midoriya's encyclopedic knowledge and lightning-fast reflexes, and the crowd erupted in cheers.

"Question eight! What does Present Mic call the devoted listeners of his show, *Put Your Hands Up Radio*?"

Ding-ding.

"Mic-ies!"

"Question fourteen! Just after her debut, the commercial that sent Mt. Lady's popularity skyrocketing was for—"

Ding-ding.

"Lady Hair shampoo and conditioner! And the tagline was 'For beautiful, shiny hair.'"

"Question twenty-five! In Laundry Hero: Wash's commercial, what does he—"

Ding-ding.

"'Washashashasha!' And he says it five times total!"

Heading straight for victory, the unrivaled Midoriya was giving off an unusual aura. With bloodshot eyes and a tinge of bloodlust in his voice, he sat stone still except to slap the buzzer (for every single question, without fail) with laser precision and focus. The audience couldn't help but shudder in mild horror.

"Not exactly a good role model..." said Togata with a straight face as he shielded Eri's eyes from the ghastly sight.

"And our final question! All Mi—"

Ding-ding.

An eerie tension fell over the audience. Midoriya had barely let the quizmaster start the question before dinging in, and when he answered, he did so slowly, with a deadly serious expression on his face.

"Seven minutes and thirty-one seconds."

The audience was confused by the cryptic answer to the unasked question. The quizmaster gulped.

"The question was, 'All Might's legendary debut video clip was how long, exactly?' And...yes! Seven minutes and thirty-one seconds is correct! Our undisputed winner is Midoriya, of class 1-A!"

"Woo, I did it!" yelped Midoriya, transforming instantly from bloodthirsty quiz demon back into his usual chipper self as he accepted the autograph board.

"How'd you know...just from 'All Mi—'?" asked Uraraka.

"Clearly the fanboy god walks among us," remarked Asui.

While the older girls seemed a little repulsed by Midoriya's fanaticism, Eri gazed up at her champion in admiration and said, "That was so cool." The boy returned her smile with an awkward one of his own.

UA

At that moment, Kyoka Jiro and Momo Yaoyorozu were buying commemorative Cementoss tumblers. They were planning to meet up with Mina Ashido and some others later, but while that group was traversing class C's haunted house, Jiro and Yaoyorozu were browsing the lane with the food carts and stalls.

"They did a great job making these drink holders!" said Jiro.

"And they appear to be selling quite well," remarked Yaoyorozu, glancing around and seeing plenty of other students holding the tumblers.

The girls started sipping through the straws and realized that the tumblers were prefilled with coconut water.

"Coconut? What's the connection between Cementoss Sensei and coconuts?" asked Yaoyorozu.

"None that I can tell," said Jiro.

Still, the slightly sweet drink brought smiles to their faces. Looking for a spot to relax and drink, they wove through the crowd and sat on some nearby stairs. As they watched the milling crowds, Jiro and Yaoyorozu suddenly felt totally at ease, to the extent that they would've turned incredulous had someone reminded them that they'd put on a live musical spectacular just that morning.

Their first real breather all day. In that moment, it hit Jiro that their big performance was really over and done with. She stretched her back and let out a sigh.

"I was kinda worried I couldn't pull it off, at first... But I'm glad I went through with it," she said.

Seeing Jiro looking so relieved put a grin on Yaoyorozu's face, but her expression quickly clouded over.

"I was...a bit disappointed," she said.

"What? Why?" asked Jiro, shocked at Yaoyorozu's declaration.

"Well...I would have loved to see you singing from the front row, Jiro."

"Huhh?"

A visibly embarrassed Jiro scowled, and her "Earphone Jack" earlobes fidgeted, as if confused.

"And yet you were still a sight to behold up there in the spotlight, even if I could only view you from behind..." said Yaoyorozu, now grinning again. "So yes, it was all very worthwhile."

"Cut it out, you," said class A's blushing rock

goddess, using one shoulder to nudge Yaoyorozu, who—still smiling—leaned in.

UA

Meanwhile, Ashido, Denki Kaminari, Minoru Mineta, and Toru Hagakure were quaking in their boots in class C's haunted house.

"Whose bright idea was it to try out a place called 'Labyrinth of Doom'...?" asked Kaminari.

"Yours, Kaminari!" said Ashido.

"Get offa my leg, Mineta!" yelped Hagakure.

"Can't help it... Too scared..." said Mineta.

Kaminari and Hagakure had thought "Why not?" initially, Ashido had been looking forward to it more than anything, and Mineta had only tagged along with 100 percent dirty intentions. However, his big mistake was underestimating how spooky a haunted house put together by amateurs could be.

The backstory was that this old house had seen its resident family slaughtered in grisly fashion fifty years back, and class C had spared no attention to the realistic details. The floorboards creaked as visitors walked through, and mountains of dust and cobwebs spoke to the house's decrepit state. Even the crude crayon drawings on the wall—which might have come off as adorable in any other setting—took on an ominous feel.

"Yet, even half a century later, only the eldest son's body remains missing… Though the house stands vacant, neighbors claim they can feel an unearthly presence emanating from its walls…"

Upon hearing the weighty narration at the start of the experience, the four members of class A—not yet scared out of their wits—had been mildly impressed. But then came the falling ax. And the door slightly ajar, behind which someone or something was peering. And the grandfather clock that wailed like a baby. And the red, infant-sized handprints staining the corridor that gradually traveled up the walls until they filled every surface. By that point, the group was trembling, and any pervy thoughts in Mineta's mind had been cleanly replaced by pure, unfiltered terror. After Hagakure ripped the clinging Mineta off of herself, he scrambled over to Kaminari and held on to his friend's leg for dear life.

"W-whaddaya say we throw in the towel...?" suggested Mineta.

"H-how, exactly?" said Kaminari. "Walk back down this hall in reverse? That'd be just as scary."

Hitoshi Shinso was eavesdropping on the terrified group from up in the ceiling crawl space.

"Shinso, those class A kids are coming your way. Scare the pants off 'em, 'kay?"

"Roger that," said Shinso with a wry grin, ready to play the part of the murdered son.

His classmates were observing from behind the scenes, feeding timed cues to the jump-scare actors via walkie-talkies. Nearby, the one in charge of dripping blood from the ceiling gave Shinso a thumbs-up before setting about their own task.

Drip...

"Huh? Is that blood...?" said Kaminari.

Drip... Drip... Drip drip...

"Why's there blood raining down on us?" said Mineta.

Drip drip drip... Drip... Drip drip drip drip drip drip drip drip drip...

The blood gushing from the ceiling soaked the

floor, leaving the group frozen in place. That was when Shinso—covered in fake blood himself—flopped from a ceiling panel to hang upside down, right in their path.

"Take me from this plaaaace…" he moaned.

"Gyaaaaaah!"

"Whoa, really?" said Shinso.

He'd been doing his best to scare them, of course, but their extreme reaction had caught him off guard and made him break character. Without even pausing to think, the group of four ran through the rest of the house screaming, half in tears.

"This Labyrinth of Doom is baaad news!" cried Mineta as he ran.

The screams faded. Shinso and his classmates were stunned yet thrilled to have scared members of class A so effectively.

"Now they know that General Studies means business too," said Shinso with a smile.

Once outside, the four scare victims collapsed in a heap, but after a quick breather, Ashido and Hagakure laughed and said, "That was awesome!"

Nearby, Mashirao Ojiro was up against an obstacle course. It was a race against time, featuring a number of creative hurdles including a steeply warped wall. Hanta Sero and Eijiro Kirishima had already run the course, and beside them stood Katsuki Bakugo, looking as sour as ever.

"Up...I go!" grunted Ojiro as he tackled the final obstacle, the warped wall. His "Tail" Quirk gave him the extra boost he needed to push up and over and press the timer button on the dais above.

"Fifteen seconds! Same time as me, dude!" shouted Kirishima.

"Looks like I win!" said Sero, chuckling. "Me and my thirteen-second record."

Sero's handy "Tape" Quirk had allowed him to sail past the obstacles with ease. All three boys had done well, but they hadn't even come close to touching the best time posted at the registration desk, which was an impressive five seconds.

"You're next, Bakugo! Show us what you're made of!" suggested Kirishima.

"What a pain. Nah, cuz even without trying, I know

I'd win," spat back Bakugo, who stood up and started to walk away. But a nearby conversation caught his ear.

"Y'know that best time? I heard it was All Might who set the record."

"Wow! When he was a student here, you mean?"

"Yup. And nobody's touched that record since. There's no beating All Might, I guess."

Upon hearing this, Bakugo spun around and glared, as if to say, "Who says I can't beat him?"

"Aw well, let's just go check out the food stalls... Huh, Bakugo? Oh, you're giving it a shot after all!" said Kirishima, seeing his friend stomp over to the registration desk without a word. Ojiro—who had missed the earlier exchange—rejoined the group and nonchalantly asked, "Bakugo's gonna try?"

Standing at the starting line, Bakugo stretched his arms and wore one of his trademark indomitable grins.

"I'll be the one to beat All Might's record, just watch me."

The starting buzzer sounded, and he was off. Bakugo vaulted over the initial obstacles with ease, clambered up the warped wall, and smashed the timer button.

"Well?" he said, supremely confident.

Ten seconds.

"The hell? That timer's gotta be busted! Lemme try again."

Unwilling to accept defeat, Bakugo ran the course again, but All Might's record time was still out of reach.

"Grr! One more time!"

"I... But... Argh! Again!"

"How'd that guy manage *five seconds* anyhow?"

Despite dozens of attempts, the coveted five-second record remained unassailable.

"How about you call it a day?" said Ojiro.

"The more tired you get, the slower you're gonna go!" said Sero. Both boys had noticed Bakugo wearing himself out and were concerned for their classmate, but Bakugo said "Shaddup" before racing back to the starting line yet again.

"I've gotta be the one to beat All Might's record!" he said, a bundle of pure determination.

"That's our Bakugo! So freaking manly!" said Kirishima, moved almost to tears by this passionate display of guts.

Bakugo would keep running the course until closing time, shouting "Lemme try tomorrow!" when they finally had to shut the operation down.

Elsewhere, Yuga Aoyama hummed a tune while munching on his Pont l'Évêque cheese. As he strolled down the lane of food stalls, he spotted Mezo Shoji and Rikido Sato running a takoyaki stand for some reason.

"Bonjour! ☆ What brings you two to be doing this?" he asked.

"Oh, hey, Aoyama," said Sato. "We ended up in charge of this little operation for now."

"One of the Business Course classes started this stand, but there's a more popular takoyaki place right over there," said Shoji, pointing with one of his "Dupli-Arm" tentacles. "Business wasn't doing well, so these guys decided to run off to hold a strategy meeting and scout the competition. We happened to be walking by, and they asked if we could hold the fort."

Aoyama glanced where Shoji's tentacle was pointing and saw a crowd lined up for a different takoyaki stall.

"How terrible! ☆ So you agreed to hold the fort, but why are you actually preparing the takoyaki?"

Surely enough, Shoji and Sato were clad in aprons

and grilling up takoyaki. While the former adroitly poured the batter into the molds, the latter deposited chunks of octopus and other ingredients into each little pool. Shoji then used another dupli-arm to flip the cooking balls, as needed.

"Well, they told us we could do some cooking if we wanted," explained Sato. "Shoji's a big fan of takoyaki to start with, and I was in the mood anyway."

"Uh-huh," agreed Shoji as more of his dupli-arms popped the finished balls out of the mold, drizzled them with sauce, and topped them with bonito flakes and dried seaweed.

"Want some, Aoyama?" he asked.

"Non. ☆ My cheese is plenty for me. ☆ Are you only cooking takoyaki, though? I smell a sweet aroma."

"Since we're here, I figured why not make some choco-yaki too. Want one?" said Sato, holding up a takoyaki-sized cake pop covered in chocolate.

"*Non,* ☆" repeated Aoyama. "I have my cheese. ☆"

"Cheese, huh… Can I get a piece?" asked Sato.

"You wish to try some? Here, if you must. ☆"

But instead of eating the Pont l'Évêque, Sato popped the morsel of cheese into one of the pools of takoyaki batter. When the ball was done, he offered it to Aoyama.

"Tell me how it tastes."

"If I must, ☆" said Aoyama, looking mildly shocked but agreeing to try the culinary creation.

"Ow, oww!"

"Well, of course the cheesy-yaki's still gonna be red hot," quipped Shoji as Aoyama struggled to swallow the snack without burning himself.

"Hmph. My cheese is as delicious as ever. ☆"

"You can just admit it's good, y'know," groaned Sato.

By this point, a number of other students had gathered, attracted by the smell.

"Did you just say 'cheesy-yaki'?" asked one of them. "Lemme get one of those!"

"Hey, me too."

"I'll take the chocolate one."

"But we're just filling in for now..." said Shoji, trying to turn away the potential customers.

"Why not let them eat what we've made so far, at least?" suggested Sato. "Who knows? Maybe they'll enjoy what we're offering."

Sato's Quirk gave him a power boost every time

he consumed sugar, so his hobby of cooking sweets (which he had a knack for) had a practical side to it. And there are no sweeter words to a chef's ear than "That was delicious." Intuiting Sato's mind-set, Shoji relented and said, "Fine."

But their takoyaki and choco-yaki were tastier than even they knew, and the blend of savory and sweet aromas wafting from the stall worked as effectively as word of mouth. Before the two boys knew it, they had a crowd of customers lined up to place orders, forcing them into production overdrive to satisfy the demand. Aoyama left them some more of his cheese as thanks and attempted to leave, but the mob had him blocked in.

"Hmph! I cannot pass! Form an orderly line, you rabble! ☆"

"Hey, thanks for taking over line-management duty, Aoyama!" shouted Sato over the din.

UA

Just as the Business Course students were returning from their strategy meeting to find that the takoyaki business was booming, Tenya Ida, Shoto Todoroki, Fumikage Tokoyami, and Koji Koda were riding a miniature locomotive in a pint-size amusement park area.

"How amusing! Wouldn't you agree, Todoroki?" said Ida.

"Sure. Feeling kinda cramped though," said Todoroki.

Which made sense, since these attractions were typically rented out for children's events. Besides the train, there was also an incredibly short roller coaster and a panda-themed ride that might have been plucked from the roof of an old department store. Ida—who tackled even amusement in a serious way—was determined to enjoy every attraction available.

"Wonderful! Let's take photographs over there next!" he declared, pointing to a novelty photo board with holes cut out over an image of the U.A. school building and Principal Nezu's face.

"Which cutout would you prefer, Todoroki? Our fair school or our esteemed principal?" asked Ida.

"Does it really matter?" groaned Todoroki.

"I suppose not. But since I'm taller, I will assume the role of the school."

Ida and Todoroki stuck their faces through the panel while Tokoyami used their phones to snap a few pictures.

"Now I will take photos for Tokoyami and Koda!" said Ida.

"No thank you..." said Tokoyami, but Dark Shadow had other ideas.

"I want a picture!" it cried.

Koda put his face through the school hole, and Dark Shadow became Principal Shadow while Tokoyami stood off to the side, looking awkward. For Tokoyami, being in proximity of the entire ridiculous affair was nearly as embarrassing as actually sticking his face through the panel.

"Fumikage! I wanna drink that!" whined Dark Shadow, noticing students carrying the Cementoss novelty tumblers. It was a fair request—they'd worked up a thirst in the course of running around from one kiddie attraction to another. While Tokoyami and Koda went off to buy the drinks, Ida and Todoroki sat down at a nearby table.

"It's quite a thing, seeing our campus so transformed," remarked Ida, excitedly surveying the scene.

Weeks of steady preparation on the whole school's part had led to this one day, so everyone present was letting loose and having fun. For one day, they could put their studies aside and even forget that this wasn't the norm. It was a welcome relief to have from time to time.

"I do hope Midoriya and the others are enjoying themselves," added Ida after a pause.

"And that girl… Eri, right? I wonder if she's having fun," said Todoroki, earning a profound nod from Ida.

The image that arose in both boys' minds was that of Midoriya growing increasingly gloomy as his work study had progressed. They now knew about how it had all gone down, roughly, and they could tell in retrospect that Midoriya had been swallowing a lot of grief, unable to put his feelings into words. Being a good friend was about more than knowing every last detail of someone's life, but Ida and Todoroki still found themselves wishing that Midoriya had trusted more in their connection.

They also knew that Eri was a big part of the feelings Midoriya had been holding back. Without a doubt, her smile would mean the world to him.

"But that Midoriya is always pushing the envelope! Like how he nearly didn't make it in time to our performance this morning. What would we have done had he failed to show up?" said Ida.

"He said he tripped and fell while out shopping," said Todoroki.

The teachers had decided to cover up Midoriya's battle with Gentle, so as far as the rest of class A knew, he'd just had an accident while out shopping for Aoyama's rope. Not that that had placated them when Midoriya showed up mere minutes before their live performance.

"It really was like 'baby's first errand,' as Sero put it!" snorted Ida, growing frustrated just remembering it. "Oh? If it isn't Ida and Todoroki."

"Hello, Tsuyu," said Ida, spinning toward the approaching group, which also included Uraraka, Togata, Eri, and Aizawa.

"What're you guys doing?" asked Uraraka.

"Tokoyami and Koda are buying us those drink receptacles in the shape of Cementoss Sensei. Wait a moment?" said Ida.

"Wasn't Midoriya with you guys?" asked Todoroki.

Uraraka made a face.

"He said he had some business to take care of," she said. "Then he ran off somewhere…"

"I dunno where Deku went..." added Eri, looking dejected.

"Don't worry!" said Togata with a wide grin. "At the speed he was going, I bet he just needed to take a tinkle! He'll be back before we know it!"

"Oh. Okay..." said Eri, seemingly aware that Togata was just guessing in an attempt to cheer her up. Observing this, Aizawa leaped into action.

"Eri, do you like cats?" he asked. "How about we try the Cat People Cafe?"

"Wait, are they cats or are they people?"

Despite her confusion, Eri's interest was piqued by Aizawa's thoughtful suggestion.

"Hey, if you bump into Deku, tell him we went to the Cat People Cafe, okay?" said Uraraka to Ida and Todoroki. As soon as the group had walked away, both boys voiced their thoughts.

"I somehow doubt that Midoriya really left them simply to use the restroom..." muttered Ida.

"Knowing him, he's probably sticking his neck into something weird again," added Todoroki.

They looked at each and realized that they were both picturing their friend diving into danger without a second thought.

"That Midoriya—I swear he doesn't know the first thing about ICE!" said Ida.

"Uhh, is that something I could help him out with?" said Todoroki.

"No, not *ice*. I-C-E. An acronym standing for 'inform, communicate, explain.' When he dashes off without informing us where he'll be, communicating with us along the way, or explaining what's happening, naturally we're prone to worrying! Like in this instance! Baby's first errand, indeed!"

"He just forgets when he's in a hurry," said Todoroki. "Maybe we could try tracking him with GPS?"

"But he often leaves his phone behind, as is the case now. We'll need to put him in the habit of remembering it!"

"Guess so."

How could they race to their friend's aid in times of trouble without knowing his location? Their frustration was palpable, though of course it came from a place of caring. There was more to friendship than keeping constant tabs on a friend, but that didn't mean that Ida and Todoroki weren't concerned for Midoriya,

as a mother might be. In the meantime, Tokoyami and Koda returned with the drinks.

"Coconut! Yummy!" said Dark Shadow, clearly in a good mood.

"Glad you like it," mumbled Koda.

"What's the matter with you two?" asked Tokoyami, sensing that something was off.

Ida explained that Midoriya had once again run off on his own, and Tokoyami said, "We just saw him running toward the dorms."

U/A

"Hey, guys, what's going on?" said Midoriya as the group of boys ran up to him in the Heights Alliance kitchen. On the counter beside him was an apple, a bag of sugar, and a small bottle of red food coloring.

"What's going on, Midoriya, is that when you sneak off to the dormitory on your own, you must inform somebody! That's what's going on!" chided Ida.

"What is the apple for?" asked Tokoyami, who immediately noticed his favorite food on the counter.

"Well, you see…"

Midoriya explained how he had promised Eri—another apple lover—a candy apple, but according to the festival pamphlet, there were no stalls selling them. So he had bought an apple during his shopping excursion that morning and returned to the dorm to prepare the treat.

"I see… So this is all for that little girl," remarked Ida.

"She was really looking forward to a candy apple, so I just had to make it happen somehow," said Midoriya with an awkward grin. Ida and Todoroki glanced at each other, and their mutual smiles seemed to say, "What are we going to do with him?" Of course their friend had once again run off for someone else's sake, so their exasperation looped back around to pride and admiration.

"So the girl is fond of apples… She and I might get along," said Tokoyami, looking intense.

"Yes, you have that in common!" said Ida, nodding and remembering the time he and Tokoyami had eaten apple pies at a theme park. "You could be apple-loving chums!"

"But can you really make a candy apple, Midoriya?" asked Tokoyami.

"It's simpler than you'd think. Even I can't screw

this up, probably. Look!" said Midoriya as he loaded up a candy apple tutorial video on his phone. The video showed someone sticking a chopstick into an apple, boiling a batch of sugar water, adding red food coloring, and finally dipping the apple in the sugary mix until it was coated.

"Ooh," said the group of boys, impressed with how simple the process seemed.

"I started to panic when the convenience store didn't have the red dye, but then it turned out Sato had some on hand."

"I would expect no less from our resident confectionary master!" said Ida.

"Red eye? Like a flight that leaves late at night?" asked Todoroki.

"Not red *eye*! Red *dye*! Like food coloring," explained Midoriya. "All right, time to do this," he added, pumping himself up. Sensing Midoriya's determination to brighten Eri's day, the rest of the boys stood by and encouraged him.

"Be careful not to stab the chopstick all the way through," said Todoroki.

"Midoriya! The sugar solution has started to

boil!" said Ida.

"Here's the dye, yep," offered Dark Shadow.

"Spin the apple carefully now..." said Tokoyami. "Like a dance at a banquet of darkness."

"It's done!" exclaimed Midoriya.

His candy apple, with its glossy red coating, looked just as well made as one from any festival stall. Upon inspection, the group was satisfied with the final product.

"Whoops, gonna be late! I'd better run!" gasped Midoriya, glancing at the clock.

"Godspeed!" said Ida.

"Don't trip and fall again, or it'll all be for nothing," added Todoroki.

As he ran, Midoriya turned back, smiled, and waved to his friends.

Outside, the setting sun had dyed the sky as red as the candy apple he held.

U

The School Festival, with all its excitement, was over. The stalls and booths and equipment—still warm from

use—lay scattered throughout the school building and across the grounds outside, but cleanup could wait until the next day. After that, life would be back to normal at U.A.

Once he'd delivered the candy apple to Eri, Midoriya started walking back across the silent grounds to the dorm. He felt a slight tingling pain in his fingers—mild inflammation. It was similar to the pain in his heart, he found himself thinking.

What had become of Gentle Criminal and La Brava after their arrest? Midoriya recognized that his life might have gone the way of Gentle's had he not encountered All Might that fateful day, so he found himself wishing only good things for the criminal who had fought so very hard.

While heroes got to bathe in the light of glory, standing in their shadows were countless men and women who'd reached for those lofty heights and failed. That's why heroes couldn't afford to lose. That's why heroes had to shoulder so much and always be ready to race toward someone in need.

With that determination driving him, Midoriya clenched his aching fist.

UA

"Hi, guys," said Midoriya as he stepped into the dorm, and the group hanging out in the first floor common area welcomed him in.

"Well, Deku? Was Eri thrilled?" asked Uraraka, who'd heard about the candy apple.

"Mm-hmm," said Midoriya with a smile.

"How wonderful, Midoriya!" said a beaming Ida, joined by Todoroki.

"Thanks for helping me out earlier. Wait, what's that smell?" said Midoriya, noticing a sweet scent wafting across the first floor.

"They're ready, everyone," said Sato, carrying out a platter of candied apples, strawberries, mikan, grapes, and other fruit. The cute, colorful assortment of bite-size treats practically popped off the plate, like something out of a fairy tale.

"Wow, what prompted this?" asked a shocked Midoriya.

"We were gifted all this fruit," explained Sato, "as thanks for helping out at the takoyaki stall. And since

you made that candy apple earlier, I thought, why not do the same with all this, for everyone?"

"It's a candied fruit wrap party!" said Ashido, hopping into the air with Hagakure at her side. Nearby, Mineta chuckled ominously.

"If you ladies like, I've got a special candied banana just for you! One condition, though! You gotta focus real hard on *licking*. No teeth..." he said, guffawing as he approached the girls.

"Lick your banana yourself," said Asui, using her own tongue not to lick, but rather to lash out some punishment.

"Ooh, which one do I want?"

"I'm going for a strawberry!"

"Gotta be an apple for me."

While most of the class leaped up to choose a fruit, Bakugo alone remained seated on the sofa.

"Don't want any, dude?" asked Kirishima.

"Sweets? Not my thing," said Bakugo with venom in his voice, but Sato walked over and offered him a long, slim red treat.

"Thought you'd say that, so I whipped up a candied chili pepper!" said Sato with a wink and a thumbs-up. Everyone knew that Bakugo loved spicy food.

"Quit going outta your way for me! And what's the point of mixing spicy and sweet?" said the enraged Bakugo, detonating a small explosion in the palm of his hand.

"C'mon, the big guy made it just for you," said Sero, grabbing the pepper and forcing it on Bakugo. From a few paces away, Midoriya watched the scene play out with a nervous smile.

"Hey. Deku, you dweeb…" said Bakugo, approaching his classmate. "Didja give that obstacle course a shot?"

"Huh? Which obstacle course?"

"Apparently, All Might set a record that nobody's ever beaten," explained Ojiro. The color drained from Midoriya's face.

"Eh? I never heard about that! You're saying All Might himself once ran this course?"

His stunned expression was that of a fan who'd missed the opportunity of a lifetime. Meanwhile, Bakugo's satisfied smirk only twisted the knife deeper.

"Bakugo challenged it over and over and over all day, but he still couldn't beat All Might's record," said Kirishima, looking disappointed.

"Nobody asked for the exposition!" said Bakugo, shoving Kirishima before turning to point the pepper at Midoriya.

"Listen—you're gonna give it a try at next year's festival, so then I can beat All Might's record *and* yours."

"Great! But I won't go down without a fight!" said Midoriya, stepping up to Bakugo's challenge with clenched fists. Beside them, Ida leaped up and clapped his hands together decisively.

"You both mean to challenge All Might's record? Spectacular! Why don't we all attempt it? That will serve to engender a competitive spirit that motivates us and creates a greater sense of unity within the class! It sounds like this obstacle course could further our education as future heroes!"

"Great idea, Ida!" said Kirishima.

"No better motivation than a record to beat," added Sato.

"I might...be interested in such a challenge..." said Tokoyami.

"Athletic Grounds Gamma would be perfect for obstacle course training," suggested Uraraka.

"Sounds like it'll do wonders for my waistline!" said Hagakure.

"Everyone…" said Yaoyorozu. "Planning for next year is all well and good, but why don't we officially bring this year's festival to a close first?"

"Fair enough. I'm ready to eat this fruit," said Asui, staring intently at her chosen treat.

With fruit in hand, class A formed a circle; Kirishima even yanked a reluctant Bakugo over.

"Ahem, in preparation for today's festival," began Ida, "we all sacrificed days' worth of time, energy, and sleep. However, it feels like only yesterday that we struggled to decide what our featured event would be… When we were unable to choose, Aizawa Sensei stepped in, scolded us, and…"

"Skip the flashback, man!" blurted Kaminari. "Keep it short and sweet!"

"Pardon me," said Ida, clearing his throat again and lifting his fruit. "Short and sweet, yes… Amazing work, everyone! Cheers!"

"Cheers!" echoed the group, treats held high. They finished the pseudo toast by chowing down and enjoying the blend of sweet sugar and slightly sour fruit as it melted in their mouths.

A delicious blend befitting this season of their youth.

Part 6
All Festivaled Out

"**A** festival without any major problems? That's something to toast to... Cheers!"

Present Mic took it upon himself to lead the toast, prompting the other teachers of the Hero Course to raise their cans of beer.

"Cheers!"

They sat in the dorm designated for U.A. educators, a structure no different from the student dorms, which meant it also had a spacious common area on the first floor. This was a handy spot for meeting up with students outside of the classroom, but the teachers often used the space to kick back and unwind. Tonight, it was the site of a casual wrap party for this group of ten, though Power Loader was off celebrating the successful tech exhibition with his Support Course students.

If class 1-A's youthful toast was marked by sweet and sour notes, the adults' toast had a bitter edge to it. In light of the heightened security that year, the exhausted teachers were filled less with a sense of accomplishment (as the kids were) and more with feelings of relief that the event was over.

"Cheers especially to you, Hound Dog! Great work today!" said Present Mic.

"Uh-huh," grunted Hound Dog, raising his can. He alone had been in charge of patrolling the perimeter of the campus all day and—now released from guard dog duty—was all too happy to let the beer work its magic.

"Dog tired, huh? I bet you'll sleep good tonight!" said Vlad King, at Hound Dog's side.

"On that note, my bed is calling me," said Shota Aizawa, who stood up to leave as soon as the toast was finished.

"Our little par-tay has only just begun, though!" said Mic, tugging Aizawa back.

"What happened to 'a quick toast and that's it'?" asked Aizawa with a scowl.

"A wrap party's all about giving thanks and reflecting, aided by a boozy haze," said Midnight,

who had drained her first can of beer and was already reaching for her second. Beside her, Thirteen held a nonalcoholic beer.

"Oh? Is that so?" he asked, genuinely curious.

"In a certain sense, perhaps," said Ectoplasm with a profound nod.

Directly across from them, All Might sat in the center of a sofa sipping his own nonalcoholic beer.

"Besides, tomorrow's a day off," added Midnight.

"Except that we have to supervise the cleanup effort," grumbled Aizawa, but he was interrupted and drowned out by Present Mic's "No sticks-in-the-mud allowed!" Utterly defeated, he sat back down and redirected his attention to the beer. That was when Aizawa first noticed how quiet All Might was being.

"Ahhh…"

Midnight let out a long, spellbound sigh.

"Is there anything greater than the School Festival? The preparation, the big day… It's what youth is all about. Racing emotions, tested friendships, naive passion… And it all comes together for that one stall, performance, or whatever… If only the festival were every day."

"Every day a festival? When on earth would the children find time to learn anything?" asked Thirteen, again in earnest.

"Once a year is the perfect frequency," said Aizawa, nodding and taking sips of his drink.

The students could go all out precisely because it was only an annual event—a singular, valuable experience that allowed them to devote themselves to having fun, if only for a spell.

"The kids really outdid themselves this year," agreed Vlad King with a hearty nod.

The teachers would get to experience the School Festival every year for as long as they worked at U.A. High, but as far as the students were concerned, it was three times only. It was a heart-pounding spectacle for the first-years, a chance for the second-years to reflect on what they'd learned, and one last, emotional hurrah for the third-years. As the student body changed, so did the event; every festival was unique in its own right. What never changed year to year was the students' dedication to having a blast.

This group of educators came to that realization all at once and felt their faces curve into smiles.

"Nothing in this world greater than youth," said Midnight, making herself blush.

Thirteen suddenly recalled something and spoke to Cementoss, seated across from him.

"The drink receptacles resembling you were quite popular."

"Really, now?" said Cementoss, unable to hide his delight.

"It was the Business Course third-years who made 'em, yeah? They did a right job good," said Snipe.

The tumbler design—which was a faithful reproduction of Cementoss's angular form—had been blowing up on social media all day, and the stall had sold out by early afternoon. Plenty of students had interrupted Cementoss's patrol to snap a pic with him and his miniature plastic likeness.

"Why not have the kids drinking outta *my* head?" shouted Present Mic, who'd spotted Cementoss enjoying his fifteen minutes of fame throughout the day.

"In plastic form, your hair would stab someone's eye out," said Aizawa. He wasn't wrong, but Mic retaliated by jabbing his friend with that same spiky hair.

"Nahh, that's where they'd stick the straw! Too long

to suck through, you say? That'd just give their lungs a nice workout!"

"Buzz off," said Aizawa, swatting at Mic as he might a pesky fly. Meanwhile, Midnight reached for her third can of beer, having downed her second as if it were water. Nobody remarked on her breathtaking pace because they knew that, for Midnight, this was taking it slow.

"The General Studies second-years made a batch of wonderful *yakisoba*," said Ectoplasm.

"Agreed—I'm glad we chose that for lunch," said Thirteen.

These two had had overlapping lunch breaks and had gone for the fried noodles when the students selling them had called out.

"Yakisoba goes great with beer," said Midnight idly, prompting the others to comment on the festival food they'd eaten that day.

"Those U.A. *manju* were also as good as any," said Cementoss. "So perfectly compact and round."

"I tried the sausage, and let me tell you—crispy on the outside, juicy on the inside. Mm-*mmm*," said Snipe.

"Sausage… Another great pairing with beer," said Midnight as she drained her fourth can.

The rest of the group chimed in, singing the praises of the crepes, the grilled corn, and so on. The conversation about food stalls sparked Vlad King's memory.

"Hey, Eraser," he said. "I spotted Shoji and Sato cooking up takoyaki. What was the deal there?"

"Huh? First I'm hearing of it," said Aizawa with a scowl, not all too happy that a pair of his students had been moonlighting without his knowledge.

Maybe just doing someone a favor?

"Well, it was some damn good takoyaki," said Vlad before drinking more of his beer.

"Takoyaki, too..." said Midnight, midchug. "Great with beer."

"Are you hungry, by chance?" asked Thirteen.

"Not starving, but I could use some snacks."

"We do have some of Lunch Rush's premade small dishes in the refrigerator, you know," added the thoughtful Thirteen, before getting up to bring said dishes from the nearby kitchen. The school chef had already prepared food for the next day, which included this assortment for the refrigerator in the teachers' dorm. In this sense, both students and staff were fueled by Lunch Rush's healthy offerings. Tonight, though, the delicious snacks helped the beer go down easier.

"Just a quick toast," they said. *Yeah, right.*

Aizawa wasn't actually surprised that a party proposed by his heaviest-drinking colleagues on a Saturday night had turned into a prolonged affair lengthened even more by the appearance of food. He told himself that he'd find an excuse to slip away as soon as possible.

But what's with him?

Something was off about All Might, who hadn't said a word since the drinking began. The man couldn't consume alcohol, but usually he would do his best to humor the boozehounds and at least smile awkwardly once they got their claws in him. Tonight, though, he sat silently, gazing at the floor and taking tiny sips of his nonalcoholic beer every so often.

"Oh, and Snipe!" said Vlad King. "I heard how you laid waste to that shooting gallery from the Support Course third-years!"

"No restraint at all? How deliciously immature of you," quipped Midnight.

"They set that up solely to square off against me, so I had to go in guns blazin'," said Snipe, in his own defense.

Throughout the conversation, All Might remained silent, and now Present Mic took notice too.

"Yo, All Might! What's with the shrinking violet act all of a sudden? When'd you turn into a wallflower?"

This got Cementoss's attention as well.

"Is everything okay?" he asked with genuine concern, turning to All Might. The latter finally looked up and realized all eyes were on him.

"Oh. Sorry," he said, still looking gloomy.

"Our colleague is dispirited over the incident concerning Midoriya of class 1-A," explained Ectoplasm.

"Ahh," said the others in understanding. They had heard how Izuku Midoriya—whose Quirk resembled All Might's—had fought with a rogue planning to disrupt U.A.'s School Festival. When the festival had begun and Midoriya still hadn't returned from his shopping trip, All Might had grown understandably distressed.

"Again, he shouldered that burden all alone instead of reaching out for help…" muttered All Might with a deep sigh, which seemed very out of character.

"Are you getting tipsy on this alcohol-free stuff?"

asked Midnight as she reached for All Might's can to double-check the label. Beside her, Aizawa adopted a grave expression and voiced his opinion.

"Yeah. Just like a certain hero we all know."

Aizawa was frustrated in his own way, but not nearly as much as Hound Dog, who stood with a start.

"I say the boy's homeroom teacher and assistant homeroom teacher are grrrrr! Your student, your responsibility bow-wow-wow!"

As the school life supervisor, Hound Dog was known for his strict ways, but his harsh attitude came from a place of love and his drive to prioritize student safety. At the time, Midoriya had done his best to downplay the epic battle against Gentle Criminal, but Hound Dog's sharp nose had sniffed out how serious it had really been. His rage now exploded at the two men most responsible for the boy's safety, and in the face of that anger, they could only apologize.

"Sorry…" muttered Aizawa.

"There's no excuse…" added All Might.

"Grrrr!"

"Hound Dog, buddy—sit down, drink your beer, and relax," said Vlad King, giving his nearly frothing

colleague some pats and rubs on the back. The school life supervisor chugged the beer in one go, as if to quench the fire within him.

"The boy's mother trusted me with him," said All Might, "so earlier, when I was wondering if something really had happened to him...I felt the way I imagine a parent does all the time. No, I'm sure even that was only a small taste of how an actual parent must worry..."

All Might recalled his promise to Midoriya's mother and felt his determination grow anew. Across the table, Midnight gave her colleague an earnest smile as she popped open another of her countless beer cans.

"You just described being a teacher," she said.

The responsibility of watching over a person raised with care by another. No amount of worrying would ever be quite enough, because for these teachers, the students they witnessed growing up day by day were as near and dear to them as children of their own.

"Yes, we must care for them," said Thirteen, nodding and getting worked up. "But worrying alone won't help them mature. We must be as strict as drill sergeants in the classroom!"

"You? Strict? I can't picture it, space boy!" mocked Present Mic.

"Nonsense! I can be unforgiving when the situation demands!"

"It's all a matter of carrot and stick, right?" said Midnight. "I could give you lessons sometime."

"I believe in your case it's more like carrot and *whip*, Midnight," came Thirteen's calm rebuttal.

Seeing the rest of the group grin at this little exchange, All Might nodded and said, "Yes…I guess you're right." Students would never grow up right if the adults in the room could only ever worry, and that applied to the teachers as well.

"I'll try harder, Aizawa!" declared All Might.

"At what? Where's this coming from?" said Aizawa.

"I mean, as a teacher!" said All Might, taking the first big swig of his drink that night.

"Don't knock yourself out," said a surprised Aizawa, muffling his retort with his beer can.

Cementoss suddenly remembered Aizawa's newest charge.

"How was little Eri's day?" he asked.

"I think she had fun. With Midoriya and Togata around, she was able to relax," said Aizawa. The group sighed in relief, and Thirteen said "Thank goodness!"

with one hand at his chest. This sparked a conversation about whether Eri should live on the first floor of the teachers' dorm or have her room next to Aizawa's, or what have you.

"As we will be having a small child living among us," said Ectoplasm, "we will need to mind ourselves more than ever, going forward."

"That's right—we gotta set good examples for the girl," agreed Hound Dog, who had finally cooled his head and who apparently thought himself the school life supervisor for the teachers as well.

"I'll do my best to teach her which men to fall for and which to avoid like the plague," said Midnight.

"I think you're failing the role model litmus test already, Midnight," warned Cementoss flatly.

Midnight chuckled. "Joking! Obviously. But for real, we'll need to buy a whole wardrobe for Eri... Oh. Right."

Everyone but Aizawa flinched at the mention of Eri's clothing and—after a pause—began to tremble. Present Mic stood up and broke the silence.

"Those wide-eyed kitties!" he shouted, releasing the floodgates and triggering a round of laughter.

"Ugh, why'd you have to remind us?" said Midnight.

Mic was referring to the clothing Aizawa had bought for Eri when the nurse at the hospital had said she needed an outfit for going out and about. As a cat lover, he'd chosen an extremely tacky sweater and matching bottoms, both covered with frills and images of cartoonish cats with sparkling puppy dog eyes. The bottoms had an especially intense energy to them, since the cats on the thighs seemed to charge forward with every step. Realizing that Aizawa couldn't be trusted with matters of fashion, the nurse had picked out an adorable jumper skirt, blouse, and pair of shoes for Eri, which had no doubt saved her from unwanted attention at the festival.

"I thought my choice was just as cute..." said Aizawa.

He was unable to accept that the cat-covered clothes weren't everyone's cup of tea, but when he'd seen Eri's smile upon being presented by the nurse with the more socially acceptable outfit, he'd held his tongue.

"Hang on, maybe the guy who couldn't care less about food, fashion, and living spaces shouldn't be the one taking care of a little girl," said Present Mic. "You've been dressed in all black since as far back

as I can remember, bud! What're you s'posed to be anyway? Crow-Man?"

Aizawa's old classmate wasn't holding back, so All Might stepped up to defend the maligned teacher.

"But high fashion is supposed to be the kind of stuff you can't really wear while walking around in public. In that sense, Aizawa's choices are cutting edge."

"That doesn't amount to much of a defense," said Midnight.

"Who cares what the clothes look like as long as they're wearable..." pouted Aizawa before taking another sip of his beer. His interest in fashion went about as far as the question "Is this enough to cover my body?"

"Anyhow," said Thirteen, changing the subject, "I hear that class A's live performance was out of this world."

"Yeah," said Aizawa, his expression softening. "They tried their best for sure."

"Whoa, whoa, whoa, Mr. Humble over here! They raised the damn roof! I was planning to just pop in for a peek, but I ended up boogying 'til the very end!" said Mic.

"Weren't you supposed to be patrolling?" asked Midnight with a smirk.

"Patrolling the dance floor, sure!" retorted Mic without missing a beat.

Ectoplasm—a lover of karaoke—peered around the others to glance at Aizawa.

"I wish I could have attended. They say the music itself was amazing, and the lead vocalist, in particular, was incredible."

"A 'sexy, husky, cute voice,' as the kids put it!" said Mic.

"Ah, if only I could have heard that," said Ectoplasm, lamenting the fact that he had missed Kyoka Jiro's performance. For a second he thought about asking the girl to karaoke so he could hear this legendary voice in person, but Ectoplasm immediately decided that that wouldn't be good for a handful of reasons.

"The girl comes from a musical family, yeah?" asked Present Mic.

"Uh-huh," said Aizawa.

"When a kid's allowed to practice what they like, and when the parents encourage it, that's how you get polished talent like that. And you could tell, with the

whole performance, that they didn't want us in the audience getting bored for even a second. With the band up there rocking the house and the crowd dancing their pants off, I was ready to run up on stage and join 'em! Might've, too, if Eraser here hadn't stopped me!"

"I'm not sure why a grown man needed me to stop him from ruining a show put on by children," said Aizawa, who was getting fed up with Mic's antics.

"That's how crazy this show was!" said Mic, ignoring Aizawa's jab altogether.

Hearing this no-holds-barred praise of class A from Mic, Vlad King wasted no time in clearing his throat and interjecting.

"Yeah, yeah, class A did great. So I hear. But my class B put on one heckuva play."

"That's what they're saying," said Snipe. "The kids in that audience were hollerin' about it afterward."

"I'm sorry I missed it," said Cementoss, earning a smile from Vlad.

"Heh, my kids put together a 100 hundred percent original script from scratch. Sure, some of the plot points were forced, but apparently it was cuz they ran into all sorts of trouble backstage. These are my kids we're talking about, though, so those scamps banded together, found solutions, and saw the whole thing through! They never cease to amaze!"

Vlad drained his beer, nearly moved to tears by thoughts of class B.

This wrap party was turning into more of a recap meeting, but as Aizawa glanced around at his colleagues enjoying themselves, he decided to stay at least a little longer. These teachers had to keep their wits about them at all times for their students' safety, but getting to see those same students cutting loose was a surefire way to lighten that burden, if only a little. There was something infectious about pure, unbridled fun, after all.

"We really have the principal to thank for all this," said Midnight soberly. The others nodded in agreement, as the School Festival wouldn't have been possible without Principal Nezu's efforts. When the national police agency's demands had put him between a rock and a hard place, he had stood his ground and begged the commissioner-general to let U.A. hold its festival. That unwavering dedication to the students reminded the teachers why they were teachers to begin with,

because despite his cute and fuzzy exterior, Principal Nezu was a principled educator.

"He's in charge here for a reason," added Cementoss.

All Might nodded and said, "I can see that."

"How lucky are we? Getting to work under a boss like him!" said an emotional Vlad King, squeezing the bridge of his nose as if to physically hold back the tears. Hound Dog gave his friend a few empathetic pats on the shoulder.

The entire group agreed, and they all began expressing how grateful they were for Principal Nezu. When it came to educational issues or even problems in their personal lives, the teachers could always rely on him to help them figure things out, almost as a parent would. He was as much their teacher as they were the children's, and that earned him deep respect from one and all.

"Did he get to enjoy the festival himself?" asked Present Mic.

"He was watching over the kids as they had fun, at any rate," said Midnight.

"I only hope that we can hold next year's festival free of fear and doubt," said Thirteen.

"Agreed," said Aizawa, sipping his beer.

Midnight hung her head.

"With the reduced scale this year, we didn't even get to plan our own event."

"Oh? Do teachers usually participate?" asked All Might.

"Yeah, usually," said Midnight, popping open another beer. "Just little things, like the group gymnastics last year, or the cheer squad the year before. And the year before that was…what, again?"

"A choral performance. I wouldn't mind a repeat of that," said Ectoplasm, leaning forward. Aizawa wasn't nearly as enthusiastic about the idea.

Why don't we just scrap it permanently?

But he decided not to voice this opinion, lest he rain on any parades. All Might, in particular, suddenly seemed to have stars in his eyes.

"Interesting! The teachers never actually participated when I was going to school here," he said.

"Speaking of," said Cementoss, "what sort of things did your class do for the festival, All Might?"

"A maid and butler cafe, for one. That whole concept was just getting popular, at the time."

"My class did a routine with dominoes," said Midnight, still gulping down beer.

"Huh? You allowed customers to knock over lines of dominoes?" asked Thirteen.

"Nuh-uh, the customers lined them up, and I would be positioned at the starting point, threatening to knock them all over. Which I always would, in the end."

"Then why go to the trouble of setting them up at all?" asked All Might, clearly not getting the gist.

"There are types out there who can't get enough of being teased like that," said Cementoss in his characteristic flat tone.

"It was a roaring success, I'll have you know," said Midnight. "What about you, Cementoss?"

"I did a *rakugo* comedy sketch."

"A man as composed as you are would make a splendid performer. Did you pick a well-known routine?" asked Ectoplasm.

"Yes, it was 'Scared of Manju.'"

"How appropriate. And you, Thirteen?" asked Midnight.

"We did a botanical cafe. Filling the classroom with

plants and mist sprayers created a supremely soothing dining experience."

"That sounds great," said All Might.

"The menu was full of herbal teas and other drinks that are gentle on the body," added Thirteen.

"I wish I could have experienced it," said a smiling All Might, to which Thirteen replied, "We would have loved to have had you there." Present Mic couldn't sit by while the nonalcoholic duo had a pleasant conversation, so he grabbed Aizawa by the shoulder and butted in.

"We did a good ol' fashion haunted house! And Eraser made for one scary monster, lemme tell you! No special costume—all he had to do was stand there!"

"But thanks to your 'Monster Mash Rap,'" said Aizawa, untangling himself from Mic's arm, "it wasn't scary at all, and everyone hated it."

"What can I say? I'm generations ahead, in terms of style!"

"Oh yeah? Well, I'm looking forward to a future without *you*."

"Ouch, Sho! What's wrong with a haunted house with a little extra flair? Back me up, guys!"

"No thanks," said Midnight. "I prefer to be actually

scared." Across from her, Snipe recalled his own school festival and spoke up.

"We did a 'Duel It Yourself' Western-style saloon cafe. Guests would play the part of the lone gunslinger from outta town, and we'd have 'em catching mugs we'd slide down the bar counter, getting all tangled up with the locals, and ending things with a quick-draw duel."

"Very interesting," said Cementoss.

"Sounds elaborate," said All Might.

"My class had a choral cafe. It was delightful," said Ectoplasm wistfully.

He sure loves singing.

Before Aizawa could comment, though, Present Mic shouted across the table to Vlad King and Hound Dog.

"What about you two? We're dying to hear!"

"Drag cafe," mumbled Vlad King, as if something bitter were caught in his throat.

"Me too," said Hound Dog with a start.

"Ahh, that's a popular choice at school festivals. I remember seeing a few in my time," said Midnight.

"The girls were crazy about the idea, for some reason..." said Vlad.

"Ours was decided by popular vote," added Hound Dog.

"What's the matter, boys? That sounds like a quick, easy way to step out of your shoes and into some unfamiliar ones, so to speak."

All of a sudden, Midnight was the voice of authority on school festivals and their place in the lives of adolescents.

"Got any photos?" she asked.

Both men shook their heads with vigor, and Vlad King let out a frustrated sigh.

"Can you imagine? I took home the prize at the bodybuilding contest, and then they stuffed me into girls' clothes..."

"Oh? Like a beauty pageant for the boys? How exciting!" said Thirteen.

"Yeah, the Mister Muscles contest!" said Vlad, striking a pose.

"I see," said Thirteen.

"I've won many a beauty pageant in my day," said Midnight.

"Yeah. I bet," said Vlad.

"Since kindergarten," she added, and the others struggled to imagine a tiny Midnight at that age.

"Even in kindergarten? Really?" asked Thirteen, tilting his head.

"Of course our Midnight was the queen of the night ever since she was a tiny tot!" said Present Mic mockingly.

Midnight blushed. "All this talk has me aching to join another school festival..." she said through hot, heavy breaths.

"But we've only just..."

Before Thirteen could finish his sentence, Midnight cut him off and went on. "Yes, yes, I know. But don't you ever wish...you could go back to your younger days?"

"Totally!" said Present Mic. "Specially since we didn't get to do our own thing this year!"

Reminiscing about past school festivals felt like the key to accessing the teachers' youth, and they all nodded in agreement.

"That doesn't mean we can put on our own special festival, though," said Cementoss, who felt the same as the others but was trying to be pragmatic.

Midnight twisted around in her seat. "How about just a taste...? Oh, we could have a little impromptu talent show!"

Midnight's suggestion came as a shock at first, but as the others began to warm up to the idea, the queen of the night pounced.

"Instead of full-blown events, we could each perform some sort of party trick? Well?"

If that were all it would take to indulge that school festival itch, why not? Understanding what Midnight was proposing, Vlad King suddenly stood up.

"I'll go first..." he said. "Presenting...the muscle wave!"

He stripped off his shirt, struck a pose, and started flexing—first with one arm, then his pecs, then the other arm—back and forth in rhythm so that some unseen force seemed to be rippling through his muscles.

"Lemme hang ten on those biceps!" shouted Mic, getting worked up. "Surf's up!"

"H-how ripped!" said All Might, feeling obligated to remark on anything to do with muscles.

Midnight guzzled her beer while admiring the wave.

"Muscles are just another thing that goes with beer. Yummm," she said.

Apparently, the versatile beer could pair with just

about anything, though Aizawa's frown indicated that he clearly didn't agree.

I knew I should've snuck out sooner...

He also knew that if he tried to escape now, Midnight and Present Mic would drag him back, saying, "Show us your party trick first." Unsure how to proceed, Aizawa watched as a satisfied Vlad King finished the muscle wave, sat back down, and gave Hound Dog a friendly pat on the shoulder.

"Hound Dog's not about to let me steal the show, are you, buddy? Go ahead and show 'em...your super sniffer!"

Hound Dog's ears pricked up. "Who, me?" he said, clearly not expecting to be called out next.

"His sniffer, though?" asked Midnight. "Is that really a party trick? Or more of a trademark skill? Or just his moneymaker?"

"Nah, listen—when Hound Dog focuses, he can tell where someone's been and what they've been up to. Go on, man! Show 'em how it works!" said Vlad.

Inspired by his friend's enthusiasm, Hound Dog said "Okay" and closed his eyes, placing himself in the zone to sniff out the slightest hints of someone's goings-on.

The teachers glanced around, gestured at each other, and decided to place Snipe's hat in front of Hound Dog.

"Well, what can you tell us?" asked Vlad.

"This is...Snipe's hat. At lunchtime, he ate wieners and chili con carne, with oolong tea on the side. The kids' shooting gallery was tougher than he thought, going in. My nose is telling me he actually had to focus. And, wait... He also ate some cotton candy? Unexpected."

"The squirts asked me to sample some," explained Snipe, the shock plain on his face. The others oohed and aahed at Hound Dog's assessment.

"You're fit to be man's best friend, pal!" said Vlad, who was moved to the point of tears and already quite drunk.

"Take it easy, there," said Hound Dog, rubbing his friend's back.

Aizawa took the opportunity to shoot his hand up. "Okay, I'm next," he said.

"Whoa! Eraser, volunteering? First time for everything!" said Present Mic.

"What on earth has gotten into you?" asked Thirteen.

They all knew that party pooper Aizawa was

usually the first to call it a night, so his unexpected assertiveness put all eyes on him. He paused before speaking again.

"I'll fall asleep in exactly two seconds."

As promised, two seconds later, Aizawa's head flopped back against the couch, and he was out like a light. Even if his body couldn't escape the interminable wrap party, at least his mind could find solace in slumberland.

"Hey! Eraser! Little Sho! Power-Saver Sho! Snooze Master!"

But not even Present Mic's litany of nicknames could rouse Aizawa from his willful sleep.

"The Great Nap Escape..." mumbled Midnight, naming the party trick.

"W-well, I guess I'll go next," said All Might timidly, since those closest to him had already had their turns. "How about a killer joke from my time in the States...?"

The others turned their eyes to him, excited to hear a joke from the greatest hero of all time.

"So, I was fighting this villain, and I won—but when the cops showed up, they arrested me instead. Why, you ask? Because I'd gotten the emergency call while in the bath and didn't have time to throw on anything! Well...? Well?"

The explosive laughter All Might was hoping for never came.

"Of course they'd arrest you. Duh," said Midnight, who did her hero duties while straddling the line of acceptable skin exposure. In her mind, going full nude wasn't fighting fair, so she wasn't about to hold back how she really felt.

"That's amusing," said Thirteen, "but I'm not sure it passes as a joke..."

Thirteen's assessment and the lukewarm reaction from the others made All Might think back on his American friend, who'd roared with laughter at this anecdote.

Dave thought it was hilarious, at any rate...

A dejected All Might went back to sipping his nonalcoholic drink, and Cementoss decided to try cheering him up.

"I'll go next..." he said, before extracting a bit of concrete from the wall with his "Cement" Quirk and sculpting it into a detailed All Might statue.

"Thank you," said All Might, dabbing his tears while admiring the handiwork.

 **SCHOOL BRIEFS**

The table was already covered in an ocean of empty beer cans and at least one bottle of tequila that Midnight had somehow snuck in. Considering the scale of the event that day, there had never been a chance that this would just be a quick wrap party, and by this point, everyone besides the alcohol-free pair and Nap Escape Aizawa was beyond drunk.

"I will go next," said Ectoplasm. "My trick is Solo Canon Singing."

He walked behind the sofa and used his Quirk to create about thirty clones of himself, all lined up, and the Ectoplasm on the far end started singing the children's classic "Frog Song." A few seconds later, the next Ectoplasm began the song anew. When the first started in on the croaking section, the third began from the start, and so on, and so on, for a seemingly never-ending Frog Song that would die out and be reborn endlessly. The lyrics and the croaking—all in the same voice—wove together to create waves of noise that assaulted the others' eardrums, rattled their brains, and lured them into a froggy labyrinth where the very concept of "frog" lost all meaning and dissolved into a swirling, abstract mess. *Why are these frogs singing? What is a frog, even? When we gaze upon the frog, does the frog gaze back knowingly? The frogs are coming. They're nearly here. All while singing this merry tune.*

"Talk about surround sound!" shouted Present Mic, riling the other drunk members of the party.

"Erm…" said All Might. He and Thirteen were stone-cold sober, and to them, Ectoplasm's song came off as an uncomfortable, brainwashing noise. The endless Frog Song conjured the image of a froggy demon hopping about in puddles of blood.

"Zzz…"

The brainwashing had worked its magic on an already exhausted Hound Dog, dragging him into a deep sleep and replacing his usual fearsome, snarling snout with a slack-jawed, peaceful one.

"Enough of that," declared Midnight. "I'm next, so lend me your back, Vlad."

She stood with her beloved whip clutched in one hand, and All Might suddenly had a bad feeling about what was coming.

"Stand right here, Vlad," she said, positioning her shirtless colleague and licking her lips in anticipation. She twisted the whip around, as if priming it to do some damage.

 SCHOOL BRIEFS

"Hang on! Are you sure about this?" said All Might, fearing that this wouldn't be appropriate for all ages.

"Listen to All Might!" said Thirteen. "We understand that the rules often don't apply at celebrations like this, but please be reasonable!"

"Shut up, boys... And watch me!" said Midnight with deranged lust in her eyes.

"Urk!" grunted Vlad, as Midnight's whip connected with his muscular back.

"Oh dear!" said Thirteen, as he and his fellow nondrinker covered their eyes.

"This! Doesn't! Hurt at all!" said Vlad, who seemed to be grinning and bearing it while continuing to strike body builder poses. Finally, Midnight stopped and wiped the sweat from her brow.

"Behold my party trick: Whip Calligraphy."

Upon the smiling Vlad's back were red, raised welts that spelled out "Long Live Youth" in kanji characters.

"In-incredible!" said All Might, amazed at Midnight's stellar penmanship, or rather, whipmanship. The drunks were just as impressed, and they demanded an immediate encore.

"Oh?" said Midnight smugly. "I live to please, in that case."

She spun Vlad King around to face her before the whipping began, and this time, she wrote a request by the audience on his pecs. Accompanying this delightful whipping was another choral round by Ectoplasm and his clones—the children's song "At the Quiet Lakeside."

The song conjured images of a placid lake and a nearby lush forest, with air fresh enough to make the lungs come alive. Then, a birdcall disrupted the stillness. Cuckoo, cuckoo. Strangely humanlike. Cuckoo, cuckoo. The cuckoo's call rattled the trees and sent ripples across the lake. Cuckoo, cuckoo. Reverberating through the mind, revealing itself as a harbinger of enlightenment.

The combination of the dreamlike singing and Midnight's chaotic whipping was more than enough to strip the listeners of their senses.

But as soon as her second round of Whip Calligraphy was finished, the teachers heard a cute voice that nonetheless seemed to reverberate from the pits of hell itself.

"What do you all think you're doing?"

"P-Principal Nezu!"

The principal—having finished his report to the police—had just entered the building. The black beady eyes that always stared up at them adorably from knee height now seemed to glint like those of a savage beast cloaked in darkness.

"Our festival was a success, so I got off with only a short talking-to from the commissioner-general, but now I return to find…whatever this is?" said the principal.

Stared down at by those eyes, the drunken teachers instantly sobered up. Even Aizawa and Hound Dog were awoken by the sudden bloodlust that permeated the room. All Might and Thirteen—the sober duo—were ahead of the curve and already quaking in fear.

"The festivities end *now*."

"Yes, sir!" said the group in unison.

With that, U.A. High School's School Festival truly drew to a close, and the teachers would spend the rest of their night and then some being lectured at. Principal Nezu's glare softened at the sight of the red welts decorating Vlad King's chest, however, and he decided to cut the impending lecture time by an entire hour.

The Whip Calligraphy spelled out "U.A. Rules."

A Note from the Creator

It's novel number 4! This time, it's all about the School
Festival at U.A., with plenty of scenes that I wish I'd had the
chance to portray in the manga! Super fun and relaxing!

KOHEI HORIKOSHI

A Note from the Author

Reading the School Festival arc in the manga
felt so comforting. Izuku and friends are always
giving 110 percent with that Plus Ultra spirit, so
when they finally got to have fun like normal
high schoolers, I found myself thinking, "Well, good
for them. Isn't that lovely," like I was a distant aunt or
something. I hope you enjoy reading about what
happened behind the scenes at the School Festival.

ANRI YOSHI

MY HERO ACADEMIA:
SCHOOL BRIEFS—FESTIVAL FOR ALL

Written by Anri Yoshi
Original story by Kohei Horikoshi
Cover and interior design by Shawn Carrico
Translation by Caleb Cook

BOKU NO HERO ACADEMIA YUUEI HAKUSHO © 2016 by Kohei Horikoshi, Anri Yoshi
All rights reserved.
First published in Japan in 2016 by SHUEISHA Inc., Tokyo.
English translation rights arranged by SHUEISHA Inc.

Published by VIZ Media, LLC
P.O. Box 77010
San Francisco, CA 94107

Library of Congress Cataloging-in-Publication Data

Names: Horikoshi, Kohei, 1986- author, artist. | Yoshi, Anri, author. |
    Cook, Caleb D., translator.
Title: Festival for all / original concept by Kohei Horikoshi ; novel by
    Anri Yoshi ; translation by Caleb D. Cook.
Description: San Francisco, CA : VIZ Media, LLC, 2020. | Series: My hero
    academia: school briefs ; vol. 4 | Summary: The students of class 1-A
    pour their hearts into staging a live concert for the U.A. High School
    Festival, which could result in some quirky performances but plenty of
    fun.
Identifiers: LCCN 2019048356 (print) | LCCN 2019048357 (ebook) | ISBN
    9781974713318 (paperback) | ISBN 9781974715909 (ebook)
Subjects: CYAC: Heroes--Fiction. | High schools--Fiction. |
    Schools--Fiction. | Festivals--Fiction. | Ability--Fiction. | Fantasy.
Classification: LCC PZ7.1.H6636 Fes 2020 (print) | LCC PZ7.1.H6636
    (ebook) | DDC [Fic]--dc23
LC record available at https://lccn.loc.gov/2019048356
LC ebook record available at https://lccn.loc.gov/2019048357

Printed in the U.S.A.

10 9 8 7 6 5 4 3 2 1
First printing, March 2020

viz.com

shonenjump.com